DARK HORSES

The Magazine of Weird Fiction

AUGUST | 2022

No. 7

CONTENTS

QUESTIONS A MAN OUGHT NOT TO ASK

Elizabeth Broadbent

When he walked into Brewster's, old men in Vietnam vet ballcaps turned from their sausage and eggs. The younger crowd, dressed mostly in coveralls, stared hard over their coffee cups. He took a seat at the counter and flipped his mug. The diner at the back of the convenience store seemed too quiet as Shirley poured his coffee. "Whatchu want?" she asked.

"The special," he replied. He wore ratty jeans and a thermal shirt but his beanie hat was all wrong, and his boots came from a fancy hiking store. The other men had a hard-muscled, rough-palmed look that came with a life working timber. He was slim and soft-handed.

At least he didn't ask for cream and sugar.

I sipped my own bitter-black coffee from the other end of the counter.

Shirley dropped a plate of biscuits and gravy on his paper placemat. "You passing through?" she asked.

He shook his head. "I'm staying at the Highmark Inn," he replied, and didn't add, *a mountain pass and a world away.* "I'm hoping to get to know some folks and hear some stories."

She snorted. "We ain't got no stories in Killdeer."

He gave her a tiny smile. "I doubt that."

She ripped his scribbled bill from her pad and turned away.

One of those stupid students up here to ask questions. They came up to Killdeer every so often and said, *Tell me your local legends,* or *I heard you believe in root medicine,* or *Do you have healers here?* Dumbass questions, questions a man ought not to ask. My stomach turned. "Forget the biscuits," I called. "Just put the coffee on my tab."

Shirley didn't glance up. "Don't worry about it, Ella Lee."

I felt him watch me walk out.

I waded through the slush and mud to a little house behind Colston's General Store. Ruby's baby wanted to come too soon. "I'll bring you some things tomorrow," I told her, and laid my hands on her belly. He curled inside her, thumb-sucking and opinionated already. I had to sweet-talk him: *Stay there. Please stay in there.*

Finally, I straightened and gave Ruby that smile she wanted. "He'll stay put til I come again."

"He?" She grinned like spring had come early. Clint wanted a junior.

I nodded.

Outside, I hugged myself and shivered, fast-walking before my toes went numb, despite my wool socks and old boots. I had to get back up the mountain—Ruby needed her things. Shirley's leg was hurting again. Mattie's back was acting up with the cold and if I could manage something for Sue Ellen's migraines, she'd knit me some gloves. I never could knit—Mama always said I dropped stitches like the devil dropped cusswords.

Anyway, my babies would be getting lonely.

I stepped over the rim of slush around my truck, hopped into the driver's seat, and turned my key. The engine cranked and died.

Goddammit.

"Can I help you?" That damn student peered at me. He wasn't bad-looking—he had dark eyes and shoulder-length hair meant for pulling. They'd call him names over that hair, but I liked it.

"Can you help me?" I snorted like Shirley. "I doubt it."

"It's either a dead battery or your starter. If you're unlucky, your alternator. Can I take a look?"

Huh. He wore synthetic wool gloves, but he sounded like any man in Killdeer. I nodded at my Ford. "Go ahead, city boy."

He stuck his head under her hood and poked around. "Your battery's dead as a doornail. I can jump you, but it'll die again. Or I can take you to the hardware store, show you which to get, and put in the new one." He blushed. "I mean, if you want."

Not a bad offer, and it would save me from paying Dale down at the garage. "Pick out the battery, jump me, then follow me home and change it out?" I asked. "I'll make you something hot to eat." And maybe something else. Maybe.

He nodded. "I'm Henry Jenkins."

"Ella Lee Merle. I'm halfway up Bertram Peak—you'll have to follow me."

He carried the battery. I let him do it, then played helpless while he jumped my Ford. Before he hooked up the positive clamp, he handed me those fake wool gloves. I could've glared. I could've said I wasn't cold. But my fingers were numb and I pulled them on.

Our roads twisted like a phone cord; there were no guardrails and I didn't go slow. Henry followed right behind me, then wound down my unpaved drive like he'd learned it long ago. "Fun ride," he said, hopping out of his shiny new Explorer.

"You're a good driver." I had to hand him that.

He didn't seem to hear. Instead, he gazed at the bare-branched oaks. My babies watched him. "You have a lot of crows up here."

"Mmm-hmm." They probably wondered who the hell he was, too.

Henry shivered, and in that fluffy new coat, he wasn't cold. "Crows always scared me."

"Why's that?"

"They're carrion eaters."

I rolled my eyes. "Believe me, they'd rather not. If you change out that battery, I'll go in and heat up some vegetable soup. That okay with you?"

He was already popping my hood, half an eye on babies. "I love vegetable soup."

I left his gloves on my truck. And I was good to him in that kitchen: vegetable soup, warm bread, sweet tea, hot coffee. Lunch was finished when he knocked. He looked then looked away when I opened the door. I should've expected it. Instead of a ratty winter coat, I wore soft jeans, a tight T-shirt, and a snuggly flannel that might've belonged to my daddy once. Henry hung his own coat. He had some muscle to his chest, and his arms weren't the sticks I'd imagined.

Lunch was small talk, stupid things. He liked my soup. He was up from App State to collect folktales, no one had any luck in this area and he thought he'd try. Grew up in Charlotte. His daddy was a mechanic, which explained why a soft-handed grad student could tell a dead battery from a faulty starter. "What do you do?" he asked.

"Oh, I stay up on the mountain and keep to myself," I told him.

"No boyfriend?" He smiled when he said it.

"Why?" I asked, sweet as my tea. "You auditioning?"

Henry had white, even teeth someone had paid a lot of money for. "Maybe. You're too pretty to stay up here all alone with those crows."

"You think so?" No one had called me pretty in a long time. Too damn long. The ones who had—well, they didn't have long, dark hair or big dark eyes. They might've fixed my roof or banged a loose chair together, but they'd expected a lot of cooing and damsel-in-distress crap over it. Henry hadn't mentioned my battery, even when he'd talked about his daddy. But he'd had plenty of good things to say about my cooking. When I asked about graduate school, he didn't seem surprised to find I had a brain in my head, either.

"With that blonde hair and blue eyes? You're definitely too pretty to sit up here on this mountain alone," Henry said.

I could've used any of those Killdeer boys. But they expected coddling, even from me. More than that, I'd come up with them—we'd climbed trees and lost teeth and picked blackberries together; they were my first kisses, my first crushes, my first dances. They belonged to Mattie or Sue Ellen or Dale. They belonged to Killdeer.

Henry didn't belong in these mountains.

So I pursed my lips. I knew damn well how pretty I was and he tried, but he couldn't stop looking. "I like it up here," I told him, then stood and walked toward my room. Thank the Lord Mama had taught me to make my bed every morning. "You coming?" I called.

Henry's chair scraped on the floor. "Yes, ma'am."

I liked that boy already.

"That was unexpected." Henry sounded uncertain. We lay under my great-aunt's quilt while I combed my fingers through his hair, shiny as a girl's.

"Mmmm." He didn't need answers.

"It was nice, don't get me wrong." He paused. "I mean, much more than nice. Just unexpected. God, my professors would kill me."

I cuddled closer. He was warm under that quilt, and it was good to be warm up on my mountain, where cold worked its way into a person's bones. "Those stupid old men are a world away," I said. "Forget them."

His hand slipped down to the small of my back. "I forgot to, um, ask. Exactly how old are you?" He chewed his lip.

I tapped that pouty lip, like my mama did to me. "Stop. You'll chap it. I'm old enough to buy liquor and not much more."

"That's young to be up here all alone. I guess you got this place from your parents?"

"From my mama." My chest hurt.

"What about your father?"

I kissed his nose and said it fast, said it so I never had to say it again. "My daddy died the day I was born, during a blizzard on the darkest day of the year." I'd been hard in coming on that cold, black night. He loved my mama, and he had to choose: a life for a life. He'd chosen us. Dale and Preston Hewitt dug us out the morning after, and they found him curled naked in the snow. "His name was Lee Evans. So I'm Ella Lee."

"You have your mother's last name, then." Henry pulled me closer.

I nodded. "We do that in my family."

"Why?"

Men and their questions. "We just do. You as good a mechanic as you say?"

Luckily he shrugged, which meant yes.

"I'll talk to Dale tomorrow. You come with me. He's looking for a man and if you want to fit into Killdeer, that's the best way to do it."

Henry pulled back a little. "You think so?"

I nodded.

Then I kicked him out.

I called Henry in the morning. We met in the diner, and almost every soul in Killdeer pretended not to watch when we sat together at the counter. "You pick up a straggler, Ella Lee?" Shirley asked when we turned our mugs.

I made a sound that could've meant yes and could've meant no.

She eyeballed Henry. "I guess you want the special again."

He nodded. "Yes, ma'am."

I knew better than to talk to Henry with everyone listening, and he was smart enough not to talk to me. But Shirley asked, "You want this check separate or together?"

People craned for our answer.

"Together," Henry replied, damn him, which told everyone exactly how far we'd gone and how he felt about it. They'd find out later that morning when I took him to the garage, but that news would've taken time to travel through Killdeer, percolating, simmering just below the surface. By taking my bill, Henry guaranteed people would talk about nothing but that student sleeping with Ella Lee.

As we walked out, the sheriff, my uncle Lonny Lee, fixed me with his meanest glare. I threw it right back. He'd been there when they found my daddy. Luckily Henry didn't see.

"Why'd you have to go and do that?" I asked Henry as the store's cowbell clanged behind us. I resisted smacking him. They'd see from the windows and talk about that, too.

"What?" Henry's eyebrows met.

"Buy me breakfast."

"I thought—I thought it was the right thing to do?"

"You think they won't talk about it?"

Henry didn't look at me. "I guess they will."

"Did you think it would give you some sort of leg up?" I asked. "Don't use me like that again or we'll run you out of town so fast you won't know what happened."

That shut him up. As we slopped silently through slush, the cold seeped through my coat. "I didn't mean it that way," Henry finally told me.

"Like hell you didn't."

But I still took him to Dale. I had to talk fast, but he said he'd try Henry out for the day. Once he'd agreed, I smiled and handed him a small bag. "I know your hands get dry, working out here in the cold all day," I told him.

"That's sweet of you, Ella Lee," he replied, and we had a deal.

With him settled, I sloshed around Killdeer all morning, my hands going numb between houses. Ruby's baby had stayed settled—restless, she said, but settled. I visited Mattie, then Sue Ellen, and she promised me a pair of gloves. Shirley was wiping down the counter when I showed my face at Brewster's again. "I have something for you," I said.

She took the bag I handed her. "You brought that student in this morning."

I made another sound that didn't mean anything.

"You sure you want to mess around with him?" Her eyes were beady as a chicken's.

"You sure you want to mess around in my business?"

She opened her mouth, then shut it.

"Uh-huh," I said. "That's right."

"How'd it go?" I asked Henry when he showed up that night. Dark had dropped long ago, but he made it up the mountain without trouble.

"He said he'd hire me if I wanted a job." He started to sit.

I shook my head. "Not on my kitchen chair. You get in that shower first. I'll have dinner ready when you get out."

"You could've called, Ella Lee." He looked at his feet. "You didn't have to make me dinner or have me up here again. I don't want you to feel—"

"I wanted to. And you wanted to come. So get your ass in that shower, then come eat my chicken." I turned away. I didn't say: *This mountain gets lonely with only my babies for company. My bed will be warm tonight, and it'll be good to wake up with someone in the morning.*

"That murder of crows was watching me when I came in," he said at dinner.

I made another one of those sounds. Later, I pulled his hair.

Henry kept working at the garage. He complained he was paying for a room at the Highmark Inn he wasn't using, and I told him to move everything to my place. "I don't want to impose," he replied.

"It's not imposing." I gave him a sweet smile.

He moved in.

Of course, his questions started. I did most of my work while he was at the garage. But some things needed moonlight. At least I had a decent pair of gloves then. "What were you doing last night, Ella Lee?" Henry asked in the morning. "I woke up and you were gone. I thought maybe you were in the bathroom, but you didn't come back."

"I had things to do." I poured his coffee, then my own.

"What kind of things are you doing in the middle of the night?" He squinted at me.

I kissed his forehead. "Things you don't need to worry about."

Once in a while, Henry made some noise about those stories. "Worry about that later," I said. "You need to get to know folks better before they'll talk to you."

He passed me his cigarette. He'd started smoking Dale's Pall Malls, then buying packs of his own. I shivered as I dragged on it, and he tucked me under his arm. "If you'd let me smoke in the house—" he started.

"Nope." I took another puff. "No cigarettes in the house, and anyway, I like you hugging me."

Once I found him tugging at my root cellar door. "What's this?" he asked, dragging me from a warm kitchen into the cold. Snow crunched underfoot as he led me to the wooden outbuilding. I'd started locking it once he moved in.

I shrugged. "Herbs. I dry stuff in there."

That seemed enough for Henry, especially when I kissed him. "Come inside," I said. "It's cold and I need warming up."

"God, those crows again. You've got to get a sound machine to keep them out," Henry said as he followed me back to the house. My babies glared at him from their tree. One flapped angrily. They didn't like him.

"They live here, same as you, and don't say things like that, Henry Jenkins." I rubbed my hands together. It smelled like snow again.

He gave them a look, then shivered in that fluffy coat of his. "It's like they're judging me."

"They do when you say things like that." I pushed open the door and slipped inside, then poured myself a cup of coffee, partly to warm my fingers around the mug.

He snorted. "Crows can't understand people."

I sat in a kitchen chair my daddy had built for my mama. He'd lathed the back into rails that bumped like strings of beads. She'd sewn bright red pads for them, faded now to dark pink. Almost two dozen years later, they still kept my bony butt from aching while I shelled peas. I glared at Henry. "Planning on leaving?"

He opened his mouth, shut it, and then finally managed, "I wasn't planning on it anytime soon, but if you want me to, I'll—"

"I didn't say I wanted you to. I'd much rather you didn't." I blushed. "But if you're staying up here, you don't talk bad about those crows." I got up to stir the stew. Henry played with his placemat.

He asked too many questions. But Henry didn't watch me while I cleaned up. He helped. He showed up with little presents from the general store—stupid things, cards or candy bars. He'd give me the last cigarette in his pack. I'd brought him up there for a reason. But that's not why I kept him.

My mama had told me it happened like that with my daddy. "I made a plan to bring him up here." She laughed. "Then I spun around and realized I was in love."

Clint Junior was a month old when Shirley told me to visit Ruby. "She ain't well," she said as I turned my mug. "You need to get over there."

"She seemed fine when I ran into her at the store yesterday."

Shirley glanced at Henry, then glanced at me. "You go see her."

Ruby had two black eyes. I gently examined the bruise on her side. "He didn't break anything," I told her. "This isn't the first time, is it?"

She stared across the room at her calendar, one that came free from the feed store. "First time since the baby came. He said I have to stop nursing him."

I trudged out to my truck, then mucked back. Several days' worth of twelve-packs filled her trash can—if Clint stopped at twelve. "So he's done it before?" I asked, crouching down beside her.

Ruby pressed her lips together and looked at that calendar again.

"Put this on three times a day. It'll help it heal and stop it from hurting," I told her. "How often does he do it?"

She must've known I wouldn't stop asking. "Maybe once or twice a week but never where anyone can see. Do you have anything to dry me up?"

"I'll take care of it," I told her as I straightened up. "Don't forget that salve."

She nodded. "Thank you, Ella Lee. God bless you."

Henry came home wide-eyed that night. His lip was chapped from chewing it. "I had to take the wrecker out to get Clint Booker's truck," he said. "He slammed it into a tree. The sheriff and the coroner were there." He shuddered. "Ella Lee, I told you crows were carrion-eaters. They took out his eyes. Why the hell he had his windows open in this cold, I'll never know. But those crows were still hanging around in the trees, like they were waiting for more or something." He shuddered.

"Huh. Did you get his truck out okay?" I kissed his head.

He rested his head on my midsection and closed his eyes. "I mean, I guess we did, but—"

"Good, because his wife doesn't have another." I tapped his lip. "Don't nibble like that. You chapped your lip up. Let me get you something for that." I opened the extra pantry and rooted something out.

Henry smeared his lips and waited until we sat down to dinner before he spoke. "You have something for everything, don't you, Ella Lee?"

I tucked some of that pretty hair behind his ear. "Don't worry about it."

"The sheriff was there. Isn't he your uncle? He hates my ass. He kept asking when I was planning on leaving."

"He never liked my mama," I said.

"Why not?"

"He just didn't." I shrugged. "You know how folks get."

Ruby's bruises hadn't faded before the funeral, and makeup caked up around her eyes. Henry held my hand as we said we were sorry about Clint. Her mama hugged me around Clint Junior. "Didn't you see Ruby the morning Clint died?" He asked as we drove back up the mountain.

"Yeah," I said. "She wasn't feeling well. I sat with her for a while."

"What was wrong with her?"

"Sad, mostly," I said, which wasn't a lie. "You know how some women get after they have a baby. Especially when their husbands drink too much."

He didn't answer. I picked up his hand and squeezed it.

Goddamn him for noticing. My stomach flipped and my toes curled in my black church shoes. He had to stop asking questions. I knew Henry, and I knew he wouldn't like their answers.

By the time green began its slow creep up the mountain, Henry sat with the younger men at the diner and downed a beer with them every night. He said they teased him for keeping it to one. They'd laugh. "You got something waiting for you, all right," they'd say. "I'd run my ass up that mountain for Ella Lee too, lucky bastard."

I'd've seethed over that, hornet-mad, but when we were thirteen, I'd knocked Randy out of an oak tree and kissed him after. At fourteen, I tricked Darryl into a thicket of poison ivy, then made it up to him in the back of his daddy's pickup. Dalton and I lost it together, and I still smiled over it. We remembered each other's lost teeth and broken arms and beestings. They were mine. They were Killdeer. If they teased, I laughed along with them.

"I've got to get started on those stories," Henry said one night as we snuggled under warm blankets, skin to skin, legs tangled together. "I'll lose my funding if I don't."

"Hush. I need to talk to you about something." I'd held her close for weeks, told her stories, sang her into staying. "You'll either be real happy or real mad."

He quieted. Henry might leave, or he might stick around. One way or another, Killdeer would catch fire with gossip. I prayed he wouldn't go, this man who brought me cookies and kissed my cheek and held my hand as we walked into the diner.

He turned enough to slip a hand onto my belly. "Right there," he whispered.

I nodded.

Henry took a leave of absence from Chapel Hill.

Like all men's fights, it was stupid from beginning to end. Randy started on Dalton. Dalton started on Randy. Randy got angry, and Dalton got angrier, and they took it outside. They began with punches, then Randy picked up a broken bottle. Dalton pulled out his Bowie knife. Maybe he'd drunk too much to remember Randy had his open carry. Maybe he'd hazed out enough to think Randy wouldn't use it.

Three shots, and the boy who'd taken my virginity bled out behind Killdeer's only bar. Dalton's blood pooled in the hot summer dust. "Tell Ella Lee," he said as red trickled from his mouth.

Henry saw it, start to finish. He sped up the mountain and held me as I cried. The child wept with me.

"Why'd Dalton want someone to tell you?" he asked as he rubbed my back up and down, up and down. His shoulder had gone wet with my tears.

"Don't you worry about it," I managed between sobs.

"I want to know. You can tell me, Ella Lee."

My sobs stopped fast. "Don't ask questions," I said, and walked out back. My babies saw my tears. I lifted my arms to them and whispered words Henry could never hear. My daughter kicked. My babies rose into dark as black as their wings.

They found Randy dead in the jail's exercise yard. The coroner shrugged. Heart attack. Maybe stroke. His eyes and tongue were gone.

That's how Sheriff Lee told it down at the diner, me sitting right there. Our eyes met. That cold, dark night hung between us, my daddy's choice. My uncle hated me for that night. But he was blood, and blood was untouchable.

Henry whirled. "What'd you say?"

Sheriff Lee glanced at him. "We found him with a flock of crows. They didn't leave til we took his body away. You remember it happened with Clint Booker. Dale's father, too. Ella Lee here, happened with her daddy when we found him up on that mountain."

People glanced at each other and shifted in their chairs. No one said much of anything after that. I couldn't finish my breakfast, and Henry told Dale he didn't feel well. The baby fluttered. But Henry followed me up the mountain. He got out of his city-boy car and trailed into the house after me.

I waited. It was coming, sure as a summer storm. I could almost smell the ozone. The hairs on my neck rose, and our child kicked hard.

"I came up here looking for stories." His voice shook. "You know them all."

I didn't speak.

"You don't go sit with women. That root cellar's not for cooking."

He'd always asked questions, and he hated my babies. I should have known it would happen one day.

"You're the wise woman or the healer or the folk magician. Whatever they call you." Henry took a step back. "You're the witch."

I stared him down. "Don't you call me a goddamn witch."

"They all know it. You wanted me because I didn't." He'd wrapped his arms around himself, despite the heat. "You killed Randy because he killed Dalton. You killed Clint because he beat up Ruby. Those crows out there"—he pointed toward the dead tree my babies loved—"they tore out their eyes."

Damn my uncle to hell, because I couldn't send him there.

Henry gestured at my belly. "And that's the next one."

"Maybe that's why I liked you at first. You didn't know." He'd caught me and I couldn't do anything but tell the truth. "But it's more now."

"I dropped out of graduate school. How do I know you didn't make me fall in love with you? It's fake. You made me feel this way."

I shook my head hard. "No." My voice caught. "Henry, I would never do that. You could always leave. Anything you feel is yours."

His boots slid on the wooden floor as he backed up again. "If I leave, you'll set your crows on me. I'm trapped here. I'm like a goddamn princess in a tower, and I fathered a psychopath."

I tried to take his hand. He jerked back. "No, it's not like that. I help—"

"You kill people. You decide who dies."

"They deserved it!" I shouted, and my babies rustled in their tree. "Henry, please." Our daughter kicked and punched. "Stop. I never did anything to you. I never made you stay and I never made you fall in love with me. I could've and I didn't. Someone up here has to help people. Someone has to keep order—"

"That's not how it works!"

"That's how it works up here, and it's always worked that way." My voice went low. "You came up here for stories? That's your story, Henry. It's different in the mountains, and it always will be."

"Now that I know, you'll never let me leave." He turned. Henry walked out, and he walked straight to that dead tree.

I sucked in a hard breath. They hated him because he'd always hated them. "Don't!" I yelled, but it was too late. Henry held out his arms like Christ on the cross. Still as stone, they burst suddenly to life, like they'd waited for that moment, like they'd known it would come and they'd only bided their time.

Henry disappeared behind beating black wings.

I screamed. Deep in my belly, our child screamed with me.

STRANGE WATER

Steve Carr

Unable to get his rowboat to move in the soupy water, Lester Tarbell pulled in the oars that were coated with algae and wished he was closer to the bank of his property. He took stock of his situation; he was stuck in the middle of the lake and the bottom of his boat had caught on something.

The long shadows of twilight was creeping across the water. The air felt thick as syrup and smelled like rancid meat. Even while sitting absolutely still on the cushioned bench, sweat poured from his body. It was like being in a fetid sauna.

Light shone like beacons through the windows of his cabin that sat back from the water about fifteen yards. Night was falling quickly and the woods around the lake were being swallowed in blackness. Pinpricks of white stars dotted the moonless sky.

On the opposite bank and sitting back from the bank about thirty yards and surrounded by tall pines, was the cabin of the elderly couple, the O'Briens, but it was dark and from the look of the lawn and many shingles missing from the roof, they had not been there for a while, nor had anyone looked after their property.

It had been three years since he had been to his cabin and it too looked abandoned and made him wonder what happened to the young man, Jessie, who had been hired to keep the place up. The change in the lake was even more disturbing and unfathomable.

As he unlaced his boots he surmised he was about a hundred yards from the dock that jutted out into the lake from his property. If his heart didn't give out on him trying to swim through the muck, he figured once he reached more shallow water he could walk on the muddy bottom the rest of the way in.

Accompanied by a discordant chorus of croaking bullfrogs, he placed his boots and socks in the bottom of the boat and swung his legs over the edge. He raised himself out of the boat and into the warm, slimy water. Bobbing alongside the boat he pushed at it, trying to dislodge it from whatever it was snagged on, but the boat didn't move. He tried to think what was on the bottom of the boat that would catch onto something, and thought of nothing, but it was stuck, nevertheless. He turned and faced the glow of light coming from the cabin, then propelled his body lengthwise into the water and began to swim.

It was like swimming in sewage. He swam through floating twigs and branches, clumps of leaves, brushed past a couple of dead catfish, the carcass of a raccoon, and several pieces of clothing. At forty-seven he was still in pretty good physical shape, but his weak heart pounded in his chest with every stroke of his arms. Keeping his gaze fixed on his cabin kept his mind off the unpleasantness of the water; the taste of it was like sucking on a dirty sponge. He had no idea what the distance was that he had swum when his feet finally touched bottom. Breathing hard he stepped into the soft, clinging mud and felt it cover his feet above the ankles.

Before he took a step he let out a yelp. "Damn, what was that?" he said aloud.

He reached down into the water and felt the place on his calf that had been bitten into. It didn't seem serious, but with mud clinging to his feet with every step, he hastily made his way to the bank and crawled onto the thick grass and laid on his back and slowly regained his normal breathing.

Standing at the window of his high-rise apartment, Lester wiped the sweat from his forehead with a wet washcloth. Looking down at the pond in the park he put the washcloth between his teeth and tilted his head back and bit down, letting the water mixed with his sweat trickle over his tongue and down his throat. He spat the washcloth out of his mouth and turned away from the window. The floor of his living room was littered with empty plastic water bottles. Kicking them aside he went into the kitchen and at the sink turned on the faucet and put his hands under it and filled his palms with lukewarm water, and then splashed it on his face. Startled, he jumped when his cellphone on the kitchen island buzzed.

He turned off the faucet and looked at the number of who was calling before he picked it up.

"Hey, Dan," he said. He listened for a moment, then said, "The trip was good. I needed the time away. I'll be into work first thing tomorrow."

He then whirled about and vomited in the sink.

Leaving the kitchen and kicking aside several water bottles he walked down the hallway stripping off his shirt and removing his pants and underwear along the way, dropping them on the floor. He went into the bathroom and turned on the shower and stepped in, adjusting the knobs so that warm water sprayed out. He stepped under the nozzle and opened his mouth and gulped down water as it sprayed his face and ran over his body.

An hour later he turned off the water and stepped out of the shower. Without drying himself he sat on a stool and raised one leg up onto the other. The large spot where whatever had bitten him was swollen and bright red. He pushed around the edges of it with his fingertips. Bright green pus oozed from it, filling the bathroom with a noxious odor. As he had done several times already since returning from the lake, he got the bottle of peroxide from the medicine cabinet and sat on the stool, swung his legs around to inside the shower, turned the water on, and poured the peroxide on the wound. The peroxide bubbled and fizzed along the perimeter of the injury as the green pus dripped into the water and circled the drain, turning the water a pale green before disappearing into it. He put some Neosporin on the spot and taped a gauze pad onto it with surgical tape.

In his bedroom he opened the drapes and then the window. He shut off the light and laid on his bed and stared out at the night sky as a continual hot breeze washed over his body.

He didn't sleep all night.

Stepping out of the elevator holding a bottled water, Lester could feel sweat trickling down his sides beneath his shirt and suit jacket. He stopped at the desk of his secretary, Toni, who peered up at him from behind her computer screen.

"Geeze, Mr. Tarbell, you look awful," she said. "Did you catch something while you were on vacation?"

"Maybe a slight bug, but I don't think it's contagious," he said. "Just to make sure, see if you can schedule an appointment for me with Doctor Ellis for this afternoon."

"Will do Mr. Tarbell. I'll tell him it's an emergency," she said as she picked up her phone.

"Thanks," he said as he opened the door to his office. He walked in and closed the door behind him and went to the large gold framed mirror hanging on the wall at the left of his desk. From the time he had left home until now, dark circles had formed under his eyes. His usually tanned face was pale and splotchy and there was a greenish tint to his parched lips.

Sitting at his desk, he turned his chair around toward the large window behind his desk, opened his leather satchel, and took out a bottled water. His fingers trembled as he unscrewed the cap, put the bottle to his mouth, and quickly drank the entire bottle. The city streets below were bustling as usual, but other than the faint hum of the air conditioning, his office was silent. He leaned his head back against the chair and looked up at the baby blue sky and tried to ignore the pounding in his temples.

When he heard his office door open he quickly swiveled around. "Hi, Dan," he said. He tossed the empty bottle in the waste basket next to his desk.

His boss was standing in the doorway. "Good Lord," Dan said. "You look like shit."

"So I've been told," Lester said. "Toni's making me an appointment with my doc for this afternoon."

Dan sat down in one of the two soft leather chairs in front of Lester's desk. "You look in no condition to go to the Anderson account meeting this morning. I'll send Laurie instead," he said.

"I'll be able to make it," Lester said.

"That's okay," Dan said. "I was going to take you off that account anyway."

"Why?" Lester asked.

"It needs a younger person on it. They're a startup company made up of twenty-somethings. Laurie is a better fit for them," Dan said.

"But I secured that account," Lester said.

"Let's face it, Lester, you're not young anymore and the Anderson account needs a fresh face working on it," Dan said.

"I'm not that old," Lester said.

"That's true but your work has been slipping lately," Dan said. "I have to put our friendship aside when I make these decisions." He paused, and then said, "It's because of our friendship I'm going to ask for your resignation before I have to fire you."

Lester felt like puking. "Just like that?" he said.

"We've been friends outside of work for too long for me to give you a song and a dance." Dan rubbed his nose and looked around the room. "What's that smell?"

Lester shifted his sore leg under his desk. "I don't know. I noticed it too. I'll have Toni call the janitor."

Dan stood up. "I hope there's no hard feelings. Go see the doctor and if you're feeling up to it I'll swim a few laps with you this evening at the club."

"I'll let you know," Lester said.

Dan left the office.

Lester scooted his chair back and rolled up his pants leg. The gauze pad over the wound was green and reeked of the odor of rotting flesh.

Seated on the exam table wearing only his boxer shorts, Lester watched Dr. Ellis at a small metal table put labels on three vials of blood.

"I'm going to have the lab analyze these STAT," Dr. Ellis said.

Lester stretched out his arm and looked at the Band Aid the doctor had put over the vein that his blood was drawn from. There was a small round reddish-green dot leaking through the pad of the Band Aid.

"That's a nasty infection where you were bitten and I think it's coursing through your entire system," Dr. Ellis said as he put the vials in a small metal basket. He turned to Lester and said, "Because of the strain this must be putting on your already weak heart I'd prefer to put you in the hospital at least for overnight so that we can monitor what's going on with you."

"I'll be okay," Lester said. "I'd prefer to take care of myself at home."

"It's your decision," Dr. Ellis said as he stood up picking up two hypodermic needles from the table. "I'll give you a tetanus shot and a shot of penicillin and I'll give you a prescription for penicillin. You can take Tylenol for the fever and any pain."

"Are you sure about what you said about the bite?" Lester said.

"I worked in emergency rooms for many years and I've seen many human bites and they looked just like the one on your leg," Dr. Ellis said.

"It happened in lake water," Lester said. "It would be impossible."

"I guess it would be," Dr. Ellis said, "but I'd bet my license that you were bitten by a human." He tore open a small alcohol pad package and took out the pad and rubbed it on Lester's deltoid muscle. He gave the penicillin shot and then the tetanus shot. "Go ahead and get dressed. I want a urine sample also. I'll give you a cup. Just give it to the nurse at the front desk when you're done."

As Lester got dressed the doctor sat at the table writing the prescription.

"If you or that bite gets any worse, go immediately to the emergency room," Dr. Ellis said. "Change that bandage on it every eight hours and keep applying the antibiotic gel to it and take the penicillin." He handed Lester the prescription.

"Okay," Lester said. He put on his tie and then his suit jacket. "You have my cellphone number to text me when you get the lab results."

The doctor handed him the urine cup. "You really should be in the hospital."

Lester walked out of the room and went into the bathroom that was down the hall. He turned on the water in the small porcelain sink and bent down and for a few minutes gulped in the warm water flowing from the faucet.

Standing at the toilet he gasped as he began to pee bright green urine into the toilet. When finished he flushed the toilet, zipped up his pants, put the empty urine cup in his inside suit pocket, and left the doctor's office.

Lester sat on the bench staring at the calm, glassy dark blue water of the pond. A child's white plastic toy sailboat sat in the middle of it barely moving. He was thinking back to why he had taken the rowboat out in the lake. He had simply been bored, nothing more.

As people passed behind him he heard snippets of their conversations, nothing of importance, just the minutiae of their daily lives. Outside of work he had no one he shared any part of his life with. He had almost married, Deana, a gorgeous magazine editor, two years earlier, but she left him saying he was "too aloof."

The late afternoon sunlight was at his back and cast a twinkling light on the pond's surface. Looking up he could see the sunlight glistening on the windows of his apartment. He wiped sweat from his face with a sweat-dampened handkerchief, and then put it to his lips and sucked on it.

His cellphone buzzed. He took it out of his suit jacket that laid next to him and looked at the text from Dr. Ellis. "Ur very sick. Call me," it said.

What Lester didn't want to tell the doctor was that with all the problems the bite had caused, it also made him feel stronger than he had felt in years. If getting well meant going back to feeling weak, he preferred being sick.

He put the cellphone back in the jacket and looked around. There was no one nearby. He got up from the bench and went to the edge of the pond and knelt down. He put one hand in the water and splashed it around, stirring up the algae at the bottom. He leaned down and put his face in the murky water and began to drink.

Leaving the park he threw the urine cup and prescription into a garbage can.

At four o'clock Lester opened the door to his apartment and was greeted with the aromas of furniture polish, glass cleaner and ammonia. Against the wall just inside the door there were four large bulging plastic garbage bags. As he entered his living room the floor was no longer littered with water bottles and every surface was cleaned to the point of shinning.

Then he heard Estella muttering to herself in his bathroom.

He placed his keys and cellphone on a table and walked down the hallway. His throat ached from thirst and his skin felt as if he had swallowed fire. At the open doorway of the bathroom he stopped and watched his housekeeper on her knees scrubbing the shower while running a steady stream of water into it. By the tone of her voice as she mumbled a litany of words and phrases in Spanish, none of which he understood, she wasn't at all happy.

"Hello Estella," he said at last.

She let out a small, startled gasp as she jumped back from the shower. She put her yellow rubber-gloved hand over her heart. "I didn't hear you come in Mr. Tarbell," she said. "You frightened me. When did you get back from vacation?"

"On Friday," he said. "I'm sorry the place was such a mess."

Estella stood up. "So many empty water bottles," she said pushing a stray strand of graying black hair back from her face with her wrist. "Everyone at the party you threw must have been really thirsty."

"There was no party," he said flatly. "How is the cleaning in here going?"

She looked at the green stain on the brush in her hand. "There is this green stuff all over everything. I'm getting it off but I've never seen anything like it. What is it?"

"Just something in the water," he said.

"It's very strange," she said. She peered at him closely. "You don't look well, Mr. Tarbell. Are you sick?"

"No," he said, then opened his mouth wide and spewed a gallon of thick, green, foul smelling liquid into her face.

She fell backwards landing on her buttocks and hitting the side of her head on the toilet. Dazed, she tried to wipe the stuff from her face as her skin began to melt. Through half opened eyes she saw blood and tissue on her gloves. "Help me," she shrieked.

As she writhed in agony on the floor, Lester removed his jacket and tie and let them drop on the floor. He then leapt on top of her and covered her mouth with his and emitted green puke into her mouth. Her neck swelled double in size and then burst. While her body still twitched, Lester got off of her and stood over her and watched her until the twitching stopped and she was dead.

"She always did ask too many questions," he said aloud as he wiped green algae colored vomit from his lips.

In the empty locker room Lester took off his clothes and put them in a locker. As he passed a large mirror in the locker room he stopped and stared at the reflection of his naked body. His skin was a pale green and dark green scales covered both his right and left sides of his torso. Raising his head he ran his fingers along two newly formed vertical slits covered by flaps of skin that ran along each side of his Adam's apple, marveling at the idea that he had gills. He ran his hand through his hair, painlessly pulling out a wad of it. He tossed the hair in a garbage can and walked through the short hallway leading to the swimming pool.

Inhaling the warm, moist air of the pool room, Lester stood in the shadows of the doorway and watched Dan taking long strokes with his arms and kicking his feet as he slowly glided toward the far end of the pool. Other than the splashing being done by Dan, it was quiet. Staying near the wall, Lester walked into the pool room and to the panel with the light switches. When he turned them off the only light on the pool was that of the dim light of night coming through the glass ceiling.

"What happened to the lights?' Dan yelled as he reached the wall at the far end of the pool.

"Dan," Lester said in a low guttural tone.

"Lester, is that you?" Dan said.

Lester went to the edge of the pool and shrouded in darkness, said, "Yes, Dan, it's me."

"I didn't think you were coming," Dan said.

"I'm here," Lester said. He stepped into the pool, immediately going beneath the surface. A moment later he popped up, spitting out a large amount of water. The chlorine was bitter and made his skin tingle uncomfortably. "Meet me in the middle," he yelled to Dan.

"Okay," Dan said.

Lester dove under the water again, and by undulating his body. he propelled himself toward the sound and vibration of Dan's movement coming from the opposite end of the pool. Once he reached what he thought was the middle of the pool he raised his upper body out of the water and took a deep breath and waited for Dan.

When Dan reached him, he said, "You must be feeling better. You got here really fast."

"I've never felt better," Lester said. "I've been thinking about what you told me in the office this morning. I'm not going to resign. I've put too much of my life in the company to resign. You're going to have to fire me."

Dan waved his arms in the water, keeping himself afloat. "I don't want to do that, but you're leaving me no choice."

"We all have choices to make," Lester said. "I just wish I could make a different choice than the one I have to make now."

"What are you talking about, Lester?" Dan said.

Lester lunged forward and threw his arms around Dan's shoulders and bit into his carotid artery.

As Dan screamed and began flailing about trying to free himself from Lester's hold, his blood became an increasingly bright red stain in the dark blue pool water.

With his teeth still in Dan's neck, Lester lowered them both under the water's surface. Air bubbles arose from Dan's open mouth as the water filled his lungs and within moments he stopped thrashing about in Lester's grip. Lester let go of Dan and swam away as Dan's lifeless body floated to the bottom of the pool.

After getting out of the pool, Lester stood in the shower and let the water wash the chlorine from his body while he gulped down the water shooting from the nozzle. He dressed hurriedly and left the building.

He stopped at the twenty-four hour convenience store and bought a case of bottled water.

Lester stood in the shadows outside the Portsman Club and watched as Deana stretched one long, tanned leg out of her car and placed the spiked heel on the sidewalk pavement. Just as she swung her other leg around and was about to place the heel of that shoe on the pavement also, he jumped out in front of her. "Boo," he said with a wide grin on his face.

She recoiled back in fear, and then seeing it was him, said, "Damn you, Lester, that wasn't funny."

"I'm trying to be more engaging," he said.

"That's being an asshole," she said. "What are you doing here?"

Lester squatted down and dangled his car keys from his fingertip. "I was hoping we could talk."

"We have nothing to talk about, Lester. I told you that when I left you." She leaned forward gazing at his face. "Are you sick? Your face is a funny color."

"I've never been better," he said. "My heart condition has gone away."

"Gone away?" she said. "Did you have surgery?"

"Something much easier," he said. He raised his pant leg and showed her the exposed, raw, pus- oozing bite mark.

She put her hand to her nose. "My God, Lester, what is that? It stinks."

"An unexpected gift," he said. "It's changed my useless, dreary life."

"You need psychiatric help. I think you've lost your mind," she said. "Now get out of my way so I can get out of my car."

Lester stood, and then placed his hands on the top of her car and blocking her in. "You might want to join me someday," he said.

"I highly doubt that," she said.

"If you do, you'll find me up at the lake. You remember, where my cabin is," he said. He grabbed her arm and bit it, hard, leaving blood forming in the toothmarks in her skin.

"Goddamn you Lester," she shrieked.

Lester ran down the sidewalk, laughing maniacally.

The hot summer air blew in through Lester's open bedroom window and washed over his naked body as he lay on his bed. Morning light began to stream in, casting the room in bright yellow light. Staring up at the smooth pale blue ceiling, he poured bottled water into his mouth. When the bottle was empty he tossed it on the floor next to his bed with the other bottles.

When his cellphone buzzed he rolled onto his side and picked it up from the bedside stand and read the text. It was from Toni and it said, "I'm in shock. Dan found dead in swimming pool. Police will be contacting you. Call me."

He got out of bed and kicked the empty bottles out of his way as he left the room and went to the bathroom. Estelle's body lay sprawled on the floor, covered in green vomit and blood. He stepped over her and peed into the toilet a large stream of green urine. At the sink he stared at his reflection in the mirror above the sink. Although his hair was gone, other than the greenish tint to his skin, he looked ill, but normal.

In his bedroom he put on a hooded sweatshirt, sweatpants and running shoes, and grabbed his car keys and was about to open the apartment door when there were several knocks on it. He looked through the peephole. Two men, one in a police uniform, were standing on the other side.

"Mr. Tarbell?" one of the two men said loudly.

Panicked, Lester glanced around the room. There was nowhere to hide. Then as he saw his reflection in the glass over a photograph hanging on the wall, an idea came to him. He removed his sweatshirt and quickly opened the door. Startled and uncertain of what they were seeing as they looked at his torso, they both hesitated just enough to give Lester time to jump on the one without a uniform. He bit into the man's throat, quickly ripping out his Adam's apple.

By the time the cop in uniform reacted by pulling out his gun, Lester was down the hallway. Just as he opened the stairwell door, a bullet ricocheted off the wall near him. He went through the door and went down the sixteen floors leaping six steps at a time. As he came out in the alley he heard sirens in the near distance. He put on his sweatshirt and walked out of the alley, across the street, and entered the park.

In the dim glow of lamplight, Lester sat on the bench and gazed at the dark motionless pond. Sirens continued to blare from the street on the other side of the line of trees that was the boundary of the park. When a teenage boy wearing a backpack and carrying a sleeping bag sat down next to him, Lester gave him a quick glance then turned back to looking at the pond.

"You from around here?" the boy said.

"Get out of here," Lester growled, still not looking at him.

"Mister, you're all green," the boy said. "Are you sick?"

Lester jumped on the boy, wrapping his hands around the boy's neck and choking him with all his strength. The boy dropped the sleeping bag and tried to fight Lester off with his fists, but Lester held on. As the boy opened his mouth, grasping for air, Lester puked green, liquidy slime into the boy's mouth. The boy stared in wide-eyed terror as Lester's vomit began to dissolve his tongue. Lester let go of the boy and stood back and watched as the boy choked to death on his own melting tongue.

Lester took off his clothes and hid them and his car keys under bushes along one side of the pond. He then took the boy's sleeping bag and backpack and shoved them in the garbage can. He removed the boy's clothes and shoved them under the bushes. Grabbing the boy's foot he dragged him to the edge of the pond. As he waded into the pond he pulled the boy with him. The pond was barely deep enough to submerge himself and the boy's body under the surface, but it would do until morning. Throughout the night he fed on the boy.

At mid-morning, Lester drove onto the gravel driveway in front of the cabin. He parked the car and got out and inhaled the stench that hung in the air. He walked around the cabin and stood looking at the lake for several minutes thinking about Deana, certain she would show up soon. He removed his clothes and ran his hands over the scales that covered his skin from his neck down to his feet. He walked into the lake, enjoying the feel of the rancid smelling water as it covered his body. He opened his mouth and gulped in the fetid water until he was completely submerged. Then he swam to the middle of the lake, and waited.

HOLY MOUNTAIN

C.J. Scuffins

I

Riley and I are feasting at Camp 2, partying in delirium with the devil, while Andrew lies unconscious in our tent.

"Andrew's sleeping his way to the top!" I say to the Sherpas with a knee-slap. Or, the Sherpas say to me with a knee-slap. Or, perhaps the Sherpas have buggered off by this point. A lot is going on, the wind's whipping us like a dominatrix, and I'm not exactly taking notes.

Between my teeth are some super-stringy neck veins, while Riley crunches down on a tasty thigh bone. After supper, we dance around the dead chap's phone, which plays only ringtones, not that anybody complains, least of all its owner.

Yet. (There's always a Yet.)

Despite the carnage, I'm not sure if Riley is truly happy.

Recent life changes have cast doubt over our future together, but I haven't found the right moment to broach the subject. Possibly, I've been too scared. Who wants to discover that your lover doesn't love you back? All the feeding frenzies in the world can't put that right.

There and then, I decide to forget about waiting for the perfect time. I have to stop being such a chickenshit. This is it! Addled or no, I lean over to ask if Riley still loves me, only to be interrupted by an avalanche.

II

It's a "common or garden-variety snowslide," according to the sniffy review in the next day's Himalayan Times. Even so, we were dumped right back down the mountain to base camp, like victims of an expertly foolish, silent movie stunt.

We had brought along a bunch of Australian men as our food source. We were lucky enough to meet them at base camp, the first time around. Leaving them buried under a ton of hard slab snow would be rude, no matter how much they wished to stay there.

Riley and I claw out every man jack, including out-for-the-count Andrew. We save the guys' lives, without anybody losing so much as a single digit. Do you think we get a single thank you?

Reading the room, I give everybody the day off. Good morale is the mainstay of any Everest expedition, but especially this one.

Since sunlight is no longer my friend, I need to ascend the mountain at night to avoid bursting into flames. There isn't an SPF high enough to protect a vampire. I know because I've tried them all, and have the scars to prove it.

Naturally, the men know that scaling the highest peak in the world is treacherous enough without venturing forth in the pitch dark, not least because they'd watched one of their climbing buddies face-plant on the Khumbu Icefall and simply slide off the mountainside. Days later, I'm convinced I can hear his dying screams ringing in my ears. Possibly because he is still falling.

I mentally message the guys with one of my patented pep talks: "Rest up for the day, chappies, and come the evening, you'll be ready to leave base camp—once more, with feeling! Remember, legendary status awaits the one or two who reach the top with Riley and me. Just think, we'll be numbered amongst the six thousand women, men and children to have conquered Mount Everest, not including Sherpas!"

That should do the trick, I think.

As for Andrew, I bade him to sleep on. He is vital to our quest, the true nature of which I am not at liberty to divulge to our Aussie companions, whom I don't want disturbed with all the deets. (They are disturbed enough already.) No, Andrew can live the dream of climbing Everest without waking.

III

Later, Riley and I sit on one of the camp's large lunar-like rocks, admiring the rollercoaster of a mountain range across the way known as Kangchenjunga.

I break the awed silence. "Andrew told me it was called Kajagoogoo."

Riley snorts.

We lose track of time. Soon, the moon lighting up the night is as full as my belly.

I whisper, so's not to raise too much alarm: "Don't look now, but it's time of the month."

Riley darts his snout to the sky, realization dawning on that handsome, hairy face. He flails a paw in my direction, as if I can help, and then slips onto the hard snow.

The werewolf is an ungainly eight-footer. His body assumes total autonomy for the duration of the transformation. Riley's mind is just along for the ride. Millions of meta changes take place within him, the science of which I'm sure would make a fascinating documentary. Outwardly, though, he resembles nothing more than a long-bearded speed freak making snow angels.

I wait the requisite fourteen minutes and forty-five seconds.

The big bad wolf fades away. Lying there in his stead is my darling girlfriend.

IV

There is no time for canoodling. My Riley needs to wrap up fast to avoid freezing to the side of the mountain.

Thankfully, she is as petite as Little Will, the expedition cook. I bade him to leave his tent and strip out of his snow clothes.

Little Will hands his garments one by one to Riley.

Once done, he looks down at himself, then up at me. "Am I going to die stark bollock naked?"

"Inappropriate," I say, and dismiss him from our presence.

While Riley dresses under the team gazebo, I catch her up on our life together.

The wolf did not leave a trace of his antics on exiting my Riley's mind. This was a great blessing, as he got up to some things that she would not approve of, to say the least. But the transformation process also left massive gaps in her own memory, which required some prompting to recall. I began with the most important matters.

"Hi, I'm your girlfriend, Mae," I say, sounding like an overconfident speed dater.

"Hi, I'm... Riley?"

"Correct. What else?"

The concentration on her face couldn't be more pained. "And... I'm... I'm *your* girlfriend?"

"Well, I hope so, or else what am I doing here?"

She smiles.

A momentous occasion.

Her pearly whites are a dazzling sight after four long weeks. I know some couples can go for ages without exchanging so much as a smirk—particularly married couples—but the absence of an affectionate smile from Riley makes every month feel like an eternity.

She snaps me out of my reverie with the question, "How did we get here?"

This is a biggie. I clear my throat. "Life started out hard for us. We were born into the same deprived, lower middle-class suburb of Dublin, Ireland—"

Riley raises a gloved hand. "Deprived of what?"

"Excitement. One of the basic human rights."

A smidgeon of a grin appears on one corner of Riley's mouth. "I'm not sure if excitement is a basic human right, but please, carry on."

I was actually being serious. But I don't let the interruption distract me from my tale: "We were on the outside, voyeurs to our own lives, not able to access the best the world had to offer. That is, until the fateful day we took a drive through the Wicklow Mountains, and found lying half-dead on the roadside, a rabid Irish Wolfhound... or so we thought... until it raised up... from the backseat of your car... and *took a bite out of you!*" I break off from the prepared script, such is the emotion I've engendered in myself. "To think, we were taking a werewolf *to the vet* when it attacked you. I mean, that was preventable—" I finger-fan away tears at the memory.

Riley takes a step backwards in the snow, as if she's received a sharp prod to the chest. "Wait... Am I now... a woman... who transforms during a full moon... into a she-wolf?"

I move into the space between us, with a reassuring smile. "No, no, don't be silly."

"Oh shit, that's a relief, I swear to g—"

"You're a he-wolf who transforms during a full moon into a woman."

The clarification has never fails to render her totally stupefied. "Seriously?... I'm a human... for one day per month!... and some kind of... wolf creature!... for the rest?"

I nod vigorously and give her a hopeful thumbs up. They call it positive reinforcement.

She begins to ugly-cry. Hard.

I take her into my arms, and do my best to ward off that most seductive and dangerous of emotions: self-pity.

Softly, I tell her, "We decided a long time ago that we have a choice: We can crawl into our shells, and never come out again, like very depressed snails. Or, we can stay out of our shells and, like super-aggressive genetically modified snails, grab the world by the balls!"

Riley pulled a face.

"Sorry... Grab the world by the gender-neutral equivalent."

"Better," she says.

"Now, which do you want to be, Riley?"

"Genetically modified snail."

"Good. Let's keep on living the life of our dreams. Starting with this."

We kiss deeper than your average Everest ice crevasse. She pulls away to look me in the eyes. Not to initiate sex, unfortunately, but to better judge my answer to her next question. The make-or-break one that never fails to rattle my rear-end.

"And how is that going? Living the life of our dreams?"

V

I compose myself.

"Living the life of our dreams is going insanely well... for the most part... Although that's not to say we don't get into the occasional scrape. Case in point, and this will make you *lol* a lot... when we visited Stockholm a while back, I was attacked by a vampire, who punctured my neck, turned me, and left me for *undead.*"

I pause for Riley's response. But there is none. Save for stunned silence. Typical. I fill the void with some other impressions from the trip. "And you know what? The vampire in question is allowed to run a walking tour in the Old Town, which we agreed is a total parody of Swedish permissiveness. I much preferred visiting the ship museum--"

Riley cuts me off with a delayed reaction: "Jesus Christ!"

I shiver violently.

She grabs me into a bear hug. "I'm so sorry, Mae."

"Not to worry, we all have our cross to bear." I shiver violently again at my poor choice of words, breaking her hold.

I stand in front of her, emotionally naked, at the most crucial moment of my story. I have to be convincing as hell--or die trying.

The matter-of-fact route has worked best in the path. Casually, I say, "But, you know, what? Our small run of bad luck is changing."

She shakes her head. "It's more like an ultra-marathon run. We should call the Guinness Book of Records."

"You might think that now, Riley... but wait until you hear this."

VI

I motion for her to sit on the rock. The stage is mine to deliver the good news.

"Something important happened on the hippie trail through Kathmandu."

Riley smirks and says, "Don't tell me, you scored some excellent weed?"

"Yes, but even more importantly, we met a spiritual guide called Andrew, who—"

She cuts me off, and isn't playing this time. "A spiritual guide called *Andrew*? From where?"

"Philly, I think."

"*Philly*? I find that hard to believe."

"Harder to believe than the vampire and werewolf stuff?"

"Frankly, yes."

"Look, I agree that Philly is an unlikely hometown for a god-bothering man, and Andrew an unlikely name, but you were very impressed with him. He swore down that he could get us into Beyul, the fabled spiritual plane of the Himalayas, rumored to be part of heaven itself, to which we can gain entry, according to Andrew, through a hidden cave entrance at the summit of the North Face of Everest."

Riley's countenance darkens. "Why are hidden entrances never at the bottom of a mountain, where they would be accessible to wheelchair users?"

"Personally, Riley, I can't speak to the accessibility issue. However, I raised it with Andrew, as you've asked that question before."

"And?"

"He doesn't know, either."

"Typical." She produces a full-on pout.

"More to the *actual point*, though, Andrew promised that Beyul is a place where we would be accepted with love and understanding, and could live in peace for eternity. His words exactly."

Riley makes another face. She's good at making faces. She should have been a sculptor. "Was he stoned?"

I cannot lie. "Well, he was with us. So, yes."

"It's drug talk, then." She gets down off the rock and walks in a little circle, looking all kinds of agitated. "Clearly, our judgement about people is impaired. This is not a guy we should follow. No way."

If I know one thing about relationships—and I probably did know only one thing—it is that couples need a project. Without a shared goal, you've got two individuals simply sharing a living space, and likely not for much longer, either. Our project is Beyul. Finding it, gaining access to it and being accepted into it. Or, if we aren't accepted into it, killing every creature in the after-life in a jealous rage. Either, or. I didn't care about the outcome, only the journey.

We can't bail on Beyul. I know in my heart that it would mean a return to drifting from one misadventure to another, before eventually drifting apart. The one thing in life that frightens me.

However, this is not my first clown rodeo. I reach into the stash pocket of my cloak. And I pull out a pre-rolled joint that makes the Camberwell Carrot look like a tiny cock.

Riley's frown could not be more theatrical if she was wearing grease paint.

I implore her, "Please. It helps. Trust me."

A long, loud sigh from Riley signals some kind of acquiescence. *"Uuuuuuuuuuuuuuuuuuuuuuugh."*

I move quickly, before she can follow up with an argument, unfolding a chair for her and sparking up the spliff.

After a few puffs, Riley undergoes her second transformation of the night: she becomes an agreeable person.

"Yes, it's all starting to come back. I have a feeling about Andrew. A good one."

"See? And you said we smoke too much."

"A very good feeling," muses Riley. She passes the joint back, eventually, and wants to know, "Are we still on course for Beyul?"

My relief is palpable, but I try to play it cool. "Oh sure, I've kept Andrew on ice in our tent. He'll be super-fresh when we hit the summit, in excellent condition to lead us to the entrance."

"Good, Mae, because we need to ready ourselves, too. Time to eat."

VII

I bade Little Will to bring forth his personal food rations. He arrives trying to stuff food into his face in vein. I have full control of his mind, body and glutton mouth.

Soon, Riley is tucking into a heated tin of tomato soup. I take great pleasure in watching her slurp it down. The same cannot be said of Little Will, who has a face like a man watching somebody eat his rations.

I bade him out of Riley's sight, behind the bathroom tent.

Soon after, I join him.

He wants to know, "Can I put clothes on?"

I smile and say, "Waste of time."

"Why?"

"Because you're my number one choice for a midnight snack." Admittedly, this is a hard thing to say to anybody. So I add lightly, "I can't stomach a full man at this hour."

Doesn't raise so much as a chuckle. In fact, Little Will bursts into tears.

I place an arm on his shoulder to comfort him. "Look on the bright side. No hard climb for you tomorrow."

And then I pull him close.

A few minutes later, we are interrupted by Leo, the self-described leader of the Australian climbers. He looks appalled at the sight of Little Will disappearing in front of his eyes.

Gobbling down my victims—blood, guts, bone, and whatever you're having yourself—is a habit that I'd picked up from the wolf. A perfectly natural development. Couples regularly influence one another's behaviour. Like when the wolf developed a penchant for capes.

"Take a photo for the 'Gram, it'll last longer," I snark at Leo.

He duly vomits at my feet. *"Ooooooogh... Ooooooooooogh..."* (You get the idea.)

I step out of the way. "Disgusting! Can't you see that I'm eating?!"

He wipes his dripping mouth on his sleeve. "Did you have to kill Little Will?"

I shoot back, "What's it to you?"

"He still owes me a shitload of cash for the trip."

I take Little Will's hand out of my mouth and shake it sternly at Leo. "I can end your money worries, right here and now—along with your life. Just say the word!"

He slopes off, moaning and groaning more than the dying Little Will.

However, I'm not a total monster. On a ridge close to Camp 2, Riley and I have a eulogy for Little Will.

"How would he like to be remembered?" I ask.

Riley concentrated hard. "Tall children?"

"Right, he never shut up about them." I raise aloft my Thermos cup, containing a little of his blood. "Little Will, you might have been small in stature, and a terrible cook, but *fair dinkum, mate...* you performed a minor miracle in siring the tallest children in Australia."

Riley says, "No, in his family."

"The tallest children in *his* family? That's not much of a boast--"

At that moment, two of our Antipodean travelling companions take the opportunity to scatter out of my range of control.

Icy mountain ridges have never been the best place for a chase sequence, and they aren't going to start tonight.

I cup my mouth with both hands and call to the escapees, "Don't run! Walk!"

In a matter of seconds, the pair slip and fall, first one, then the other, into an impossibly deep crevasse.

That is, impossibly deep for most rescuers—but not for me.

I push off into the sky, albeit a little unsteadily, due to the altitude. Soon I am upright and drifting through the rarified air with ease. Just like riding a bike.

After floating into the icy hole of death, I locate the men waist high in a sub-zero pool of water. I drop them at their tents like some kind of stork, but for grown Aussies. Throughout the short flight, they beg me to be left to die. Next level ungratefulness.

Riley taps Little Will's watch. "Why are we still standing around? Let's go find the entrance to Beyul."

Sometimes the woman frightens me more than the wolf.

I take her aside for a quiet word—I had flown into the crevasse with less trepidation. "Sorry, Riley, it's almost morning, and I'm not a morning person, because one burst of sunlight and I'm basically flame grilled. We can climb tonight, if that's okay with you?"

She does not look happy.

VIII

The first light of dawn--you absolute bastard!--is visible in the sky.

Riley sees it. She knows I have to seek refuge.

"Oh, for god's sake," she says. "Fine!"

She stomps across the snow into our tent.

I follow at speed, albeit feeling terrible. I pride myself on being able to give Riley everything that she wants.

Imagine my surprise, then, when I crawl into our blow-up bed to find Riley giving me exactly what *I* want: the look.

A month has passed since we are last intimate and, seemingly, Riley is feeling the need as much as me.

I spring into action and bid sleeping Andrew to spend the night on the toilet.

After which, Riley and I have a free tent. We take the opportunity to indulge in some terrific tent sex. Dirty and sweaty and using our favourite new toy with the wireless remote. The best tent sex in living—and undead—memory. In fact, if the Nepalese government presented an award for the best tent sex of the season, we would pick up the winning trophy. But, hey, this isn't a campsite in the south of France.

Easily, it is our most tender moment on the climb. (I will be tender for days after, too.) After this, how can I not feel incredibly optimistic about our relationship? Maybe this trip will be the making of us.

There is only one way to find out for sure.

While in a post-coital doze, I screw up my courage, and lean over to ask if Riley still loves me, when I realize that I am spooning the wolf.

My Riley is gone. One day, and done. It hits me harder than usual.

To add insult, the wolf shudders in disgust at the sight of me. He untangles himself from my legs with a couple of donkey kicks and positively vrooms out of the tent *through a hole that he rips in the side.*

Poor post-sex etiquette, to say the least.

I remember the last thing that my Riley said to me: "Just think, in one month's time, we'll be in heaven. Right?"

The question was rhetorical.

Like, no pressure, babes.

IX

Shit rolls downhill. Consequently, I apply Riley's pressure along the chain.

The next night, on reaching Camp 4, the last stop before the peak, we keep on climbing. Nobody dares move a muscle that isn't in the direction of the summit. Even the wolf is on-message, for once.

We spot boots sticking out of the snow every few hundred yards in the Death Zone. That said, the news isn't all bad. I manage to swap in a pair of technical climbers for my Doc Martens, which despite looking truly sick, are inappropriate for the terrain.

I am happy when everyone survives that weird shoe-studded trail.

Then, Leo, the money-obsessed motormouth, has to go and spoil everything by falling to his death 500 yards from the top.

"Shame," I say to myself. "I wanted to eat him."

I suspect that Riley the Wolf might have shoved Leo off the side, due to his constant carping, and I am not shy about levelling the accusation.

He roars back, denying it. I flail a dismissive arm in his direction. The wolf does likewise. A regular Han and Chewy tribute act, we are. I shake my head and chortle.

The chuckle catches in my throat when, suddenly, the wolf takes a mighty leap into an icy canyon after Leo.

At my shoulder appears Garrett, for whom I've had soft spot since overhearing some of the men call him, 'Speccy Garrett', on account of his bottle-end glasses. (Those men are no longer with us.) I had worn spectacles in my childhood but, since becoming a vampire, all my medical issues had cleared up, save for the murderous blood lust. Still, I identified, and always made time for him.

He wants to know, "Is Riley attempting to save Leo?"

"No, I suspect he's going to do something unspeakable to his corpse."

"More unspeakable than eating it?"

I nod gravely.

Garrett tries to sneak a peek.

I cover his eyes. "Best not to look. Come on."

We traipse a little further up the ridge.

"I've never met a vampire before," he says. "I'm a big fan of the books and movies, though. Do you mind me asking how are you turned?"

"A funky old bloodsucker from the 17th Century got me in Sweden."

"Sorry to hear that."

"I'm not totally innocent, to be honest. Riley had become a wolf-woman, and I thought, 'Well, how's this going to work?' I'd never heard of a bar scene dedicated to women and wolves, for example. Of course, people change over time, but the person I loved had become an eight-foot hairball overnight. It was hard to get my head around."

"I can imagine."

"Can you?"

"No, not really."

"But instead of working through it with Riley, I ran into the arms of another person. The totally wrong person. That is one holiday romance that will stay with me forever."

I pull down my turtle neck to reveal the fang bites.

He takes a good gander. "They're kind of cool."

"Thank you. Less off-putting than a neck tattoo, I suppose."

He says, "And it must have been fascinating to meet a person from the Age of Enlightenment, yes?"

"No. She isn't enlightened in the slightest. Never took the time to learn modern ways."

"Such as?"

"Such as brushing one's teeth. Breakfast Breath, I called her."

We both chuckle.

"Did you try to teach her basic hygiene, Mae?"

"No, I added her to my list of motivations for drinking. She taught *me* something, though: How to make mediaeval jam. I stir honey and grape pulp in a cauldron over an open fire for several hours, until it's got the texture and consistency of feces. Looks like it, too." I smack my lips. "*Buono!*"

There is a short moment of silence before Garrett says, "Right, I see."

The wolf rejoins us.

"Oh, it's you." I throw him a haughty look. "Will you have the energy for the climb after your exertions down there?"

The wolf mouths what I'm sure is a gross obscenity.

A shadowy figure appears ahead of us, adding to the mountainside's air of spectrality. What is this fresh hell?

X

"*Yoooo,* Mae!" the figure hollers. "Guess who's up and at 'em?" A pair of thumbs are silhouetted in the half light. "This guy!"

Andrew stands above us on the ridge. The first time that he's appeared in the open of his own volition. Sometimes, I lost mesmeric control of familiars during tent sex. The price of doing business.

Andrew steps closer, all smiles. "I heard you both sniggering like schoolgirls. What'cha laughing at?"

Garrett says, "An ex-lover with halitosis that Mae called Breakfast Breath!"

"Ha!" Andrew advances on us, looking as jolly as Father Christmas on Ecstasy.

He looks to be carrying a flagpole.

Within a few feet, I can see the pole properly. The blood-stained flag atop read, *The Michigan State Corpses.*

Earlier that night, we had bumped into the flag's owners, a bunch of bros from the midwestern university. They were explaining to anybody within earshot the meaning of their ironic slogan. In response, I decided that they should die. You should never have to explain the meaning of your flag. That's the flag's job.

"Why are you carrying that stupid thing?" I ask.

His smile vanishes. "I'm gonna plant it where it belongs."

He turns the pole parallel to the ground and plunges the sharp end through Riley's midriff.

The wolf pitches forward on the pole, gasping for air.

Andrew retracts it just as violently.

Riley crashes backwards onto the hard packed snow, blood upchucking from his stomach onto the mountain floor.

I have no time to criticize Andrew's sloppy kill work because I am too busy bellowing, *"Nooooooooooooo!"*

The wolf dies instantly and begins transforming at a terrible rate.

Dropping to my knees, I cradle his massive head and rub my face against his rapidly receding facial hair. And then he is gone. I will miss the mutt.

Garrett is being angry with Andrew on our behalf. "Why did you do that? They're just a young couple on vacation.

Troubled, yes, but very well-intentioned, I'm sure. Plus, you know... cruelty to animals."

"You're talking about cruelty?!" Andrew's cheery manner has been replaced by the whining demeanor of a world-class self-pity merchant. "I've been drugged off my ass this entire trip and left to lie in a tent without so much as a hoagie for company. And for what? Feeding a line of bullshit to a couple of lesbians in a Nepalese bar in the hopes of a threesome? Like, who hasn't tried that at least once in their lives?"

I look up. "Wait! What did you say?"

"I'd high hopes of a threesome!" The words echo across the Himalayan Mountains.

"No, about Beyul! Are you saying it doesn't exist?!"

"Beyul is nothing but a myth, unlike that ugly old Yeti you got there." Andrew must have taken a class in sneering, such is his talent for it. "I'm gonna have its head mounted on my wall beside my Gritty poster. I'll be the most famous hunter in the whole wide world, and free of the goddamn daily grind of the spiritual guide." He pats the murder weapon that he'd pulled from Riley's chest. "And just wait 'til you see how much I get for this on eBay!"

In my arms, Riley is almost fully back to herself, albeit with a giant hole where her stomach had been. We have lost the wolf, and our purpose, in one swoop. I can't lose Riley, as well. Equally, I don't know how to save her.

Garrett is furious now. "You weren't drugged, Andrew. You were under the telepathic control of Mae, a bona fide vampire. You should feel privileged! And that isn't a Yeti, it is a were-wolf!"

My voice is a jaded whisper. "No, a wolf-were, or woman-wolf, or something like that."

Andrew takes a gander at Riley, seeing quite clearly that she isn't a damn Sasquatch, or even the Abominable Snowman, but a beautiful punk rock pixie.

"Aw, shitballs," he says.

I vow to make him exclaim pained expletives for the remainder of his short, miserable existence, as soon as I laid my lover to rest.

Andrew's next comment is harder to parse: "I miss haying."

Garret looks at him funny. "Haying?"

"I miss bringing in the hay," says Andrew.

"What are you talking about?!" Garrett shouts.

An explanation occurs to me: Andrew sounds like he is suffering from altitude sickness, characterized by a severe clouding of the mind, due to having woken up close to the summit without time to acclimatize.

He toddles off, followed by Garrett, who is offering the advice, "Careful, you stupid man!"

I look down at my Riley. The big shaggy beast has left behind a tear in her eye.

"We're done," she says.

And *there it is.* Riley is breaking up with me. Deep down I knew she hadn't been happy—

Riley continues, with a faint smile, "The wolf and I are consciously uncoupled."

My heart fairly bursts. Adrenalin floods my brain. She isn't talking about *me!*

With that, an idea presents itself. Something which had likely been hiding in the recesses of my mind since that horrible night in Stockholm, when I had been transformed utterly and forever.

An idea that might solve our problems, once and for all.

XI

"Time for a change," I whisper to Riley.

With that, I neck my lover, like only a vampire can. A little blood spurts onto the snow. I suck down the sweet AB Negative that gushes from her jugular. Just enough to turn her, and not a pint more.

After which, I let the unnatural take its course.

Up ahead, Andrew is lying on his back, doing a doggy-paddle. Garrett stands over the fool, trying to coach him out of his madness.

He doesn't succeed, and I can't say that I'm unhappy about it. Andrew races on all-fours to the edge of the ridge and drops off the mountain like a lemming.

Garrett shakes his head in disbelief. He shouldn't be surprised. Most of our expedition has taken the shortcut down.

Later, we have a drink for the departed, as is our well-worn custom. Such is the death toll, it is hard to believe we aren't all alcoholics by that point.

Riley the Vampire stands beside me for the eulogy. She looks less sickly, albeit permanently pale, but at least the hole-in-chest issue had cleared up.

Pointing into the white death, directly below, she kicks us off with, "Here lies fucking Andrew."

"Well, over there," I say, pointing off to the right, where both feet stick out of the snow.

Riley says, "What can we say about Andrew that isn't complete bullshit?"

I think for a moment. "Wasn't he an absent father?"

Garrett interjects. "To use the man's own words, he is "'a satellite patriarch.'"

Riley and I snort with laughter.

Garrett's demeanor remains respectful throughout.

Eventually, we stop sniggering.

And that's Andrew's eulogy done. Fitting.

Almost immediately after, anxiety takes hold. I am desperate to interest Riley in a new goal, lest she decides we no longer need each other. I have one idea. I hope that it's original enough to interest her, or I fear all is lost.

XII

"Let's climb to the peak," I say, as sincerely as I can muster. "If we can't find the way to Beyul, we could hit the summit. And maybe hit all the summits in the Himalayas. Very few people have done it, Sherpas not included."

Riley shakes her head. "I don't think so. Look at those clouds rolling in. There's a snow storm coming."

I haven't noticed it in all the commotion, but the clouds almost upon us are darker than my cold black heart. They are pure thunderheads. What was the point of trying to save our relationship, if we die in the mother of all storms?

"Okay, new mission," I announce. "Let's get the hell down this mountain before we're trapped here for eternity."

Riley does not have to be asked twice. "Agreed."

I look at Garrett. "What about the last man standing? You're welcome to accompany us on our descent?"

Riley is amused. "Two women will be travelling alone in need of protection."

He considers my offer for a moment, before adjusting his prescription snow goggles, and declares, "Thank you, but you know what? I fancy climbing the rest of the way, storm or no. I think it would be good for my self-esteem and overall confidence."

The sky holds its breath long enough for us to say our goodbyes.

I shake his hand. "Garrett, the best of Irish luck."

Riley looks at him. "You do you," she offers.

And off goes Garrett, happy as the proverbial Larry, in the direction of the storm clouds.

I turn to Riley. "Hasn't a hope in hell."

She nods in agreement. "He will be dead within five minutes."

"Pity," I note. "He might have made a good familiar. It's not too late for me to bade him to return?"

She considers it. "He doesn't value his life. I'm not sure if that's a good or bad trait in a familiar."

Further up the ridge, Garrett is heading out of my mesmeric range.

"Well, what should I do?"

She shrugs. "Let him die."

At that moment, Garrett turns back and cries, "Farewell, my friends!"

We wave him off in unison. "Bye-bye!"

He disappears into those clouds. This storm is going to be a monster.

XIII

Riley and I quickly trek down to Camp 4.

"Good to have you back," I tell her.

"Good to be back."

"Even after what I did?"

"Turned me from a dying wolf to a living vampire?" she says.

"Technically, you're undead."

"Right, and I have the marks to prove it." She rubs her sore neck.

"You're not mad?"

"Considering the alternative, no," she says.

A moment later, she is betraying more concern. "What's it like, being a vampire?"

I have to be honest. "A bit colder than being a human. Although we save thousands every year on heating bills--likewise at the supermarket. And you'll be able to fly, which means no more buses, unless you want to surf on their roofs, like I sometimes do."

"Because they traverse set routes?"

"Yeah. Nobody tells you this, but you don't suddenly become an expert navigator just because you can fly."

"Nice to hear. Because guess what? Living one day a month as a woman, and the rest of the time as a big smelly man-dog? Not a great existence. Must have been why I was so keen to believe Andrew about Beyul. I was desperate for real change. Something positive, long-lasting. Something *good*."

I am not sure if I can ever again provide *good*. But I do have one idea to help us out of our current predicament.

"You need a pick-me-up." I take her hand. "Now, watch me, and do as I do."

I levitate in the air. She follows suit. We take a moment to smooth out her shakiness. She's a quick learner. We glide down the mountain.

On reaching Camp 2, we hover well above the other climbers, taking in one last view of Everest's stunning neighbor, Kangchenjunga.

After the sublime, comes the ridiculous: Near Camp 1, we fly over the remains of our cook, Little Will.

Riley doesn't recognize him. "Wonder what happened to him? Exposure?"

"Yes, to his own food."

She takes the opportunity for a teachable moment. "You know, we have acclimated not just to the altitude, but to death."

"Is that wrong?" Genuinely, I want to know. By this point, my shared humanity is a long-distant memory.

Riley doesn't register my question. She has more thoughts of her own to share: "And I think we should only kill when we absolutely need to. People who totally deserve it. Alternatively, we should explore a plant-based diet, too."

I don't understand this madness. Killing only the suck-worthy? Looking for plant-based blood? Whatever did she mean? But I am not going to argue, as is my way. Besides, the storm has captured the mountaintop and we have to keep moving, or else. Even so, I imagine an even more frightening scenario than being buried alive under a mountain of snow: What if Riley and I had different ideas completely about vampiring? How is that going to work?

We float the rest of the way, hands by sides.

The atmosphere has changed. I can feel it.

XIV

On touching down at base camp, we discover that new expedition groups have also landed. They include the world-famous English climbers, James Culture and Alan Straddles. The middle-aged gentlemen catch sight of us, two innocent-looking young vampire women, and within seconds invite us to their marquee-sized tent for a liquid breakfast, with (to quote Straddles) "a promise for more if you fancy it."

Riley is more interested in sourcing some old-fashioned jam, for which she has inherited quite a craving. I tell her, if she can wait until we returned to civilization, I will fire up the cauldron and make a huge batch using Nepalese honey, the good stuff that makes you hallucinate wildly. She relents, and we take the men up on their offer of booze, if nothing else.

Along with bottles of wine, the chaps have started early on the bottled oxygen. Straddles takes a blast of H20 and passes it to Culture, who duly gorges himself. "Good old English air!" he says. "None of your foreign muck!"

I can't tell if Riley considers either of these old boys suck-worthy. But I am hungry after journeying down the mountain, and implore her with my eyes. She closes her own, wincing, and then reopens them with a faint nod.

On cue, we commence with the slaughter and drink the men dry, before toasting their demise with a blast of good old English air.

Crikey and what-o, but it's fun! Maybe things have not changed between us, as I'd feared on the flight down. I sense that this is the perfect moment to find out.

"Are you happy with me, Riley?"

She turns in my direction with head in hands—Alan Straddles' head—and says, "I will be happy after we store away the rest of this food. It's too much for two vampires."

This is one underwhelming reply, to say the least. "What do you mean, 'store away'?" I ask.

Riley puts Straddles' head on her lap. "I mean, we should stop feeding now. Keep the leftovers in a mini-fridge. Finish them over the next week or two." She doesn't even wait for my response, before lumping the head into a sleeping bag. "This will have to do for now."

"No!" I say.

I don't know who is more shocked at my using this word—her or me.

"Sorry?" She puts down the sleeping bag. "Do you have something to say, Mae?"

"Yes, Riley, I do! We're in the middle of a kill. Vampires don't stop mid-frenzy to bag up leftovers. We're not having baby-back ribs with fried fish in a Texas Roadhouse!"

Something inside me has snapped. Something other than one of the ribs I've wholly consumed, at any rate.

Riley dismisses me as thoroughly as the wolf had done mid-spoon the previous day. "Well, I'm stopping and bagging them up," she sniffs, while turning away. "You do what you like. Just like you did in Sweden."

I throw down the arm I'd been chewing on. "Do you not think I've paid a harsh enough price for that transgression?!"

"I'm not sure you've learned anything, to be honest. You're still the same live-for-the-moment, maverick Mae."

"But that's me. That's who I am. Do you want me to deny who I am?"

"Do it for yourself, Mae. You will never get old, but your shit already has."

Even by vampire standards, I think that is cold. "What are you saying?"

"I want you to grow up. Is that clear enough for you?"

I stand up, instead. Fists clenched so tightly that my skin turns off-white. "Riley, I asked if you are happy--"

"And I answered you."

"In a manner of speaking, you did. But you didn't ask in return if I'm happy."

"I presume that you are."

"You presumed wrong."

Riley doesn't show an ounce of emotion. The one part of being a vampire for which she's demonstrated a good instinct. She cuts the tension. "Spit it out. What's the matter?"

I stride to the other side of the tent for time to think, almost slipping on a piece of gristle as I go. I steady myself on an oxygen tank and regain my composure. "We have so much in common, Riley... And yet--"

"And yet, what?"

"I feel totally alone. I've spent so many years worrying about your happiness that I'd forgotten about my own. I need time to figure out my feelings, you know, and have the space to be the best vampire that I can be."

"Wait. You're breaking up with me?"

Silence. The wind outside howls like a banshee lamenting a death. The storm has found us.

"Yes, I think I am."

Riley bows her head and whispers, "Fuck."

She always has to get the last word. I can't argue with this one.

XV

We brave out the storm, lying side by side, hands across chests, in the traditional vampire style. But we are no longer together.

The next evening, all is calm. I pack a small rucksack.

Maybe, in the fullness of time, I will realize that I spoke too soon. That I should have sucked up Riley's harsh words, like so much climbers' blood, rather than blurting out my own in the heat of the moment.

On the other hand, us supernaturals aren't ones for relationship counselling. We're spontaneous creatures, closer to nature than humans, and closer to our own true natures, or at least we should be.

The great mountain had no doubt played its part. Its elemental conditions are mighty conducive to getting in touch with oneself, when not trying to kill you. Yes, indeed, Mount

Everest, the Chomolungma, the Mother Goddess of Earth, is a good wing-woman to have in a crisis.

In the same spirit, I will always be there for Riley, if she needs me. At this point, though, I feel she no longer does.

I don't confide how much I still need her. From the time we met, she had made all the plans, all the big decisions. From this day forward, I'll have to do that for myself. Scary.

We part at the bottom of base camp, which has never looked more like a frozen moon.

"Where will you go, Mae?"

"Home."

"Ireland? You still consider it home?"

"I want to find out." I hoist my backpack onto my shoulders. "And you?"

"I might stick around this place."

"Well, you won't starve, that's for sure."

She says, "Think I'll try to find Beyul. See if it's a myth, once and for all. And don't worry, I'll text you if I find it."

"In return, I'll keep an eye out for the highway to hell."

I receive the full glory of Riley's smile for the final time. Then, she turns away to call on a neighbor for freezer bags. There is nothing else for it. I turn away, too.

For the first time in years, I am on my own.

Except for Garrett, that is. He has gone ahead to arrange lodgings. I had bade him in secret the previous day to descend the mountain in our wake, rather than die stupidly in a storm. In time, he will come to thank me.

I take the rocky Gorap Shep trail through the brightly-colored and picturesque villages of the Sherpas. The grief of separation made me forget that I could fly.

THE DEVIL'S TRIANGLE

Wayne Kyle Spitzer

Because our days were so exhausting, I was usually out the instant I hit the pillow, entering a deep and perfect sleep the dreams of which I could not recall; on other days, the work continued—the only difference being that in the dreams I flew over the island like a hawk (rather than search it house by house, or, just as often, beach café by tiki bar); and was able to spot a bread crumb even while soaring high enough to see most of Alice Town (though not so far as Bailey Town). And always, always, I returned to the Bimini Big Game Resort and Marina, with its ruined, capsized boats and broken, shattered docks (now undulating against the seawall); its multiple floors and long, red roof—which, only weeks before, had been the only thing standing between Búi and I (and Amanda, too) and the tsunami.

Nor did I merely revisit it in my dreams, for it was where I started and ended each day's search regardless of how much of the island we'd cleared (we'd reached Resorts World Bimini—the approximate halfway point between Alice Town and Bailey Town). It was where I was at, looking at Búi's many half-filled water glasses, when I heard Amanda's voice crackle suddenly, startlingly, over the walkie: "Sebastian, I'm a few houses past Resorts World—on the state-side of the key. And, ah, you're going to want to see this." She quickly added: "It's not a body, nothing like that. It's nothing to do with Búi. Just—get over here."

I stared out across what was left of the marina; at the crystal clear water and the reddening sky—in which a solitary pterodactyl whirled—and the golden clouds, like heaps of fleece pillows. Her tone of voice had given me pause. "Sure. I—I was re-checking the Big Game. The Bar and Grill. I'll ... I'll head up right now."

And I went, hurrying to where the Jeep was parked in front of the Sue and Joy General Store and laying the flare gun on its passenger seat—before turning the ignition and heading up Bimini Bay Way, staring between houses as I drove and peering into their tall windows (although for what I wasn't sure; we'd already checked them for Búi and their original owners had long since vanished in the Flashback). It was easy to do; driving so carelessly—there weren't any other drivers or pedestrians to think about; only the Compies scattering before you like flightless gulls or the occasional newspaper or plastic bag. That's how it had been since the Event; and, as a consequence, you tended to get to where you were going quickly and effortlessly, before the melancholy of the place could really sink in (it was the seeing of it all at once that did it; the sheer totality of all that emptiness blurring past), something I was immensely grateful for as I turned left on Queen's Street and jounced onto the beach—and saw Amanda's Prius parked next to the overturned truck and custom boat trailer; next to which lay, well, whatever it was. Because it looked like a kind of miniature submarine, only shaped and painted like a shark, replete with rows of sharp teeth. It even had a dorsal fin.

"What the hell is it?" I asked, getting out, then hurried to help her as she shouldered her rifle and gripped the thing by a fin.

"Seriously?" she asked. The sand loosened and slid from its hull as we pulled the object upright. "It's a Seabreacher." She stood back and dusted her hands. "Sort of a jet ski, only enclosed. It—people use it to dive under the water ... then breach the surface, like a dolphin."

I stood and looked at it—at the Seabreacher. "Okay. Great. And this helps us—"

"Don't be obtuse." She moved forward and tried the hatch handle, which turned—then opened the cockpit, slowly. "Seats two. Might even be able to slip in a third. Knew a guy before the Flashback, said he could pilot his all the way to Miami. That's what I meant by, 'Don't be obtuse.' It means we're not stuck here."

I must have looked—unenthused.

"That's a good thing," she said. "In case you were wondering."

"A good thing," I said, and looked back the way I'd come.

"Yes, *a good thing.*"

I focused on the small church further back along the beach—Gateway Outreach Ministry—which we'd already checked. Except for the sacristy, which had been locked (this had been before we found the rifle). Wasn't it at least possible she'd taken refuge inside it?

"Sebastian ..."

The answer, of course, was no. She'd have responded when we called out (and we'd called out a *lot*). But what if she were sick, or wounded— unconscious, even? What if she'd been unable to hear us, or to respond even if she did? What if she'd been too debilitated to reach the door? Was it really magical thinking to suppose—

Amanda exhaled, defeated. "Sebastian ... what can I do?"

I turned to look at her as she shrunk down in the sand, looking more tired than any twentysomething had a right to—more haggard, her eyes vacant and puffy, her cheeks sallow. "I mean, how long do you think they'll last? One small, overgrown grocery store ... and a mini food-mart? (by 'overgrown' she'd meant the ubiquitous moss and vine—presumably prehistoric—which had come, along with the Compies and the pterodactyls, immediately after the Flashback) Six months? Couple of years—if we're lucky?"

I scanned the nearby homes. "Longer than that. Plus there's the bars and restaurants—not to mention all the houses." I looked at the darkening horizon. "It'll be light for a while. We should keep searching."

I felt her eyes follow me as I walked toward the Jeep.

"Sometimes I don't know what you want from me," she said.

I paused before climbing in. "I want you to help me find my wife," I said.

After which, realizing how cruel that had been, how unfair (for she'd been helping me tirelessly), I added, "You should get some rest. It's—it's going to be dark. I'll push on from here; okay? Don't wait up."

And I put the Jeep in gear.

The first thing I noticed when I got home to the duplex—it must have been around midnight—was that Amanda's unit was dark while mine was illuminated; something quickly explained when I swung open the door and saw the burning candles, not to mention the tinfoil-covered plate and half bottle of wine; or, for that matter, the greeting card-sized envelope—from which I withdrew a letter that read, simply, Happy 50th, S.B. *We'll find her.*

I guess I must have smiled.

"S.B." —*Sebastian Adams.* She had a memory like a steel trap.

I lifted the tinfoil and peeked at the dish—a fusilli pasta topped with white marinara sauce—but wasn't any hungrier than the last time she'd cooked; and merely re-covered it. I looked around the table. That wine, though.

I snatched it up and fetched a glass (funny she hadn't left me one) and then went out onto the deck—startling a Compy in the process, which leapt from the round table next to my chair and strutted—its little head bobbing, its tail jouncing—across the planks; into the cycad bushes.

"Boo," I said.

Then I settled in: propping my feet on the stool and looking out at the Atlantic, purposefully ignoring the little framed picture of Búi; disregarding the spilled peanuts and disturbed water glasses, some of which had been knocked over and some of which remained standing, but all of which contained or had contained small amounts of water, because now *I* was doing it (wasn't it funny, how couples could rub off on each other?).

"Tomorrow we'll do Resorts World," I said, still not looking at the picture. "If that's okay with you. I mean, it's like I've always said: You're the boss. No, no, that's how I want it. You should know that by now."

I took a drink straight from the bottle, which Amanda had left open, and exhaled. Then I tipped it again and drained the entire contents. "Well, honey, you wanted purple yams, remember? But it looks like your *dinky dau* sense of direction finally got the best of you. So you lost your way and mistook north for south; and now you're probably on the other side of Bailey Town—alone, confused, and terrified, I'm sure."

I looked at the sky—just a vast, black pit, mostly, like the ocean—but didn't see any lights, nor the prism-like jewels that had hung there since the Flashback—the time-storm; whatever—I suppose because of the clouds.

"Or ... have you disappeared to somewhere else; like everyone else on this island? Another time, another place, another epoch ..." I lolled my head against the backrest, woozily. "What the hell is this Flashback, anyway? I'll tell you what I think; I'm afraid Time itself has somehow been changed so that half the planet never existed. I'm afraid the first wave took the others and the second wave brought the dinosaurs and a third wave, well, a third wave took you. Because, honey, I've searched ... and searched ... and you just don't seem to be here. Not fucking anywhere."

A moment came and went; a moment in which I might have shattered, a moment in which I was capable of anything. But, as I said: It came ... and it went.

And then I *did* look at her picture; at her round, youthful face (although we were both precisely the same age), and her large, straight teeth. At the big brown eyes I'd often joked would eventually outgrow their sockets (to just dangle from their stalks, I'd said), and her ability to smile for the camera even after a terrifying ride in Miami (with a drunken boat captain) had almost ended our vacation—and our lives. At the girl from Bình Du'o'ng Province, South Vietnam, whom I'd married 7 years prior and experienced the initial Flashback with—as well as the meteor-caused tsunami which had happened immediately after— but who had then vanished without a trace on a trip to get purple yams. And chia seeds.

I laughed a little at that in the warm, bitter darkness, wondering if she'd ever found them.

"I bet you did," I said, my faculties beginning to fade, the wine beginning to kick my ass, before reaching out and laying the picture face-down on the table.

And then I slept, and eventually dreamed; of the island as seen from the heavens and of floating through a kind of limbo, a kind of purgatory. Of passing over Alice Town and Bailey Town and on to the open sea, which was infinite. Of being joined by another so close that our wings brushed, and flying—not like Icarus, not like Daedalus—but purposefully, fearlessly, without regret, into the ancient, seething, fire-pit cauldron of the sun.

Of what went through my mind when I saw the turkey-sized predators congregating at the end of the jetty (or rather the start, for we were heading back toward shore from the ferry terminal), I have no memory; other than to say I'd felt suddenly good, suddenly content, while striding along beside Amanda over the lapping surf (and laughing at some joke), and that, when I saw the predators, all of that just went away, just drained from the world, like the sun going behind a cloud.

Because it *had* been a good day; the first since Búi had disappeared. Nor could I put my finger on why, exactly: maybe it was simply because the weather had been so agreeable; or because the company had been so good. Maybe it was because we'd cleared an entire block of houses as well as the ferry by late afternoon and I'd been reminded of just how many places—safe places—she could still be. Or maybe it was because I'd forgotten, however briefly, that the world was a necropolis: a windswept graveyard, and that we—Amanda and I—were likely the last living souls.

Until we were coming back along the jetty from the ferry, that is. Until the slim, lithe predators with their long, dark tails and blue-gray coastal-patterns; their white, unblinking eyes, their little, undulating mohawks comprised of blood-red feathers, saw us.

"Are those—what did you call them? Comp—compsognathuses?" asked Amanda. "They don't look the same, for some reason."

I peered at the animals—just animals—through the shimmering heat: the three of them having become four, the four of them about to become five (as yet another emerged from behind an abandoned SUV) ... no, *six*.

"No," I said, absently. "I don't think so. They're too big."

I watched as the things seemed to focus on us, one of them shaking off while another used a foreclaw to scratch itself behind the ear. "Plus, they've got longer arms. And those toe claws; they're extendable—you can see it from here. More like a

deinonychus (I had a dinosaur encyclopedia back at the duplex),
or a—"

"Or a what?" She stared at the animals as though she were
seeing a ghost. "Or a velociraptor, like in *Jurassic Park?*" She
started to back up. "Because if that's what you were going to say,
don't. Besides, they're too small."

"Movies exaggerate," I said—also backing up. "Just easy
does it. They're as scared of us as we are of them."

But now there were more, about twelve at least (with still
more streaming in), one of which darted forward abruptly ... and
then hesitated, craning its neck to look at the others and
shrieking—angrily, it seemed—just like a bird.

"Yeah," said Amanda. "That's bullshit. Look at them.
There's strength in numbers."

Alas, I *was* looking at them, at their eerily intense focus (like
cats starring at a pair of robins) and their coiled shanks; at their
tails which were moving back and forth like knives.

I felt my vest for the other flares and touched the heel of
my knife. "They're going to try and rush us; we're going to have
to run for it. Are you up to it? I'm thinking all the way to the
ferry ... how about it?"

"It'll bring them on, I guarantee it ..." She unslung her rifle
and looked over her shoulder. "I don't think we can make it. I
mean—wait ... what about that island shuttle?"

I watched as the others filed after the first and they
regrouped—just a gaggle of heads and tails—then glanced at it
myself. "Forget it. It's got a canvas roof— remember?"

"With steel ribs, though."

"Yeah, but—we'd be *stuck.* There's no key."

And then they were coming, not in a gaggle but in a
staggered formation, bounding forward but in turns, running and
pausing, as we turned and flat-out bolted—sprinting for the ferry
as the sun shone hot and merciless and without compassion;
veering for the island shuttle once we realized we'd never make
it, piling through its driver's door and slamming it behind us as

the raptors fell upon the vehicle like a threshing machine and began climbing and tearing at its canopy.

"Wait, don't—"

My ears rung as she started firing, blindly, into the animals, at least two of the slugs hitting the beams and ricocheting—one of them close enough to nick my ear.

"There's too many of them," I shouted, even as a dark snout stabbed between the beams and banged to a halt, gnashing its teeth. "Just stay low, they can't get through."

After which I eased the rifle from her hands and we hunkered near the floor; the raptors screaming and tearing the roof apart even as ragged pieces of it fell and they began reaching between its beams with their human-like forelimbs—swiping at us with their curved talons, blindly; reaching and groping and searching—like zombies.

Neither of us behaved bravely or kept our wits about ourselves. It was the screams that were the worst; which tore through the air like knives—like fighter jets passing so close you could see the rivets. Which split your mind so that you were too disoriented to think, to do much of anything. I'm afraid they got the better of us both as we cowered near the floor and covered our ears; as Amanda reached for me and pulled me close and I wrapped her up in my arms and squeezed her tight.

"Just hold me," she said, as the entire vehicle rocked and shook around us. "And don't let go."

And so I held her and didn't let go; cradling her head in my hands as the raptors screamed and continued their assault—as the entire truck was lifted on one side only to crash back down, as she said almost softly, "We—we have a responsibility. I never told you. A purpose. Because ... we're the last, and someone ... someone has to continue. Do you understand what I'm saying?"

I squeezed her tighter even as the glass and canvas rained down. *"Shhh,* save your strength. They'll give up and go away ... we just have to wait. Just—hang in there."

More broken glass; more shredded canvas. I squeezed my eyes shut; I was no longer certain they wouldn't get in.

"I want you to promise me, Sebastian. Promise me you'll meet me there—no matter what. Because if not us, then who?"

The raptors cried out in unison—like a perverse choir; it was almost as though they were celebrating, like this was their victory song.

I pulled back enough to look at her; at her dark blue eyes, so much like my own, and her youthful face—which was beautiful by any measure—understanding with perfect clarity what she'd meant; and realizing, too, to my great and utter astonishment, that I agreed; that we owed the world that, every bit as much as I owed Búi. That it was our duty, in a sense ... to ensure the bloodline survived; to propagate the species. And I realized something else, now that we were so close we could smell each other's sweat and I could feel the back of her hair against my hand and her body pressed against my own—like a rock; now that I had a raging hard-on in the face of what seemed certain death, God help me. And that was that I *wanted to live.* Irregardless of if we found Búi or not; I wanted to live—to continue the journey—to spit in the eye of whatever had selected me for extinction, whatever had selected Búi for extinction, selected the *whole world.* Whatever had just crossed us out like a grammatical error: 'Remove this,' and scrubbed us from the sands of Time.

That's when we noticed it; at precisely the same instant, I'm sure. That the sound and the chaos had stopped. That the raptors, the screamers, the bloody *things,* had called off their attack. That the world had gone quiet again and we could hear the water lapping against the jetty's pilings.

We disengaged from each other and got up—looked out the driver's side window.

The majority of the horde was gone. We were still trapped; there remained about six animals—yes, six, exactly—but the larger pack, the larger pod, herd, murder, whatever, was gone.

I picked up the flare gun (which I'd found in the wreckage of a yacht after the tsunami, when Búi was still here), and unsheathed my knife. Amanda did the same, chambering a round in the Marlin rifle and taking out her own knife.

We never discussed it; never weighed the pros and cons of what we were about to do, never questioned what we were both feeling, which was that we wanted to live, and to not be afraid. We never asked the other if it was the right thing or the wrong thing—if it was worth the risk, say, when the other raptors could come screaming back at any moment. We already knew it was the right thing, because it was the only thing. Instead I just gripped the door handle and looked at her, and when she was ready—she nodded.

And then I threw open the door and we piled out.

There were six of them, as I said—all of whom rushed us the instant our feet touched the ground. All of whom snarled and charged us like wolverines as we raised our weapons and fired—the flare gun cracking and hissing, blanching the scarlet haze (for the sun had painted everything red and gold), its projectile punching through one of the raptors' chests and lighting it up so that its ribs were backlit briefly and I could see, if only for an instant, its burning, beating heart.

Yet still they came, another one leaping at me even as I dropped the gun—which clattered against the planks—as I dropped it and grabbed the thing by its neck—then brought the knife down with my other hand and stabbed it between the eyes.

"Run!" I shouted, even as Amanda shot another—her second—and then bolted toward the shore, drawing the others so that I was able to snatch up the flare gun and quickly reload it; so that I was able to pursue them and to shoot one in the back— while Amanda turned and took out the last of them (shooting it in the head so that the back of its skull exploded like a spaghetti dinner thrown against the wall; so that it collapsed, writhing, about 10 feet in front of her—whereupon she quickly approached it and shot it again, just to be sure).

And then she looked at me (as the dead and dying animals lay all around us) and I looked back: our chests heaving; our faces covered in sweat, our worn clothes bloody and disheveled, and I knew that *she* knew—which was that today *we* were the predators, the thing needing to be feared—the killers. And that neither of us needed to worry; not about food or other predators or mysterious lights in the sky or anything. Because we were the masters of our fate, we and no one else, not even God. And we were the master of the world's fate, too.

At which she ran to me and we collided and I held her fast, there on the long jetty in the Atlantic Ocean (in the Bermuda Triangle), there beneath a day moon and the blood-red sky, in an instant in which it was good, so very good, not to be afraid, not to be alone. And as to what may or may not have happened in those breaths, those pulse points between that moment and the next—the next day, the next search, the next milestone; as to that, I offer only a quote from Gandhi: "Speak only if it improves upon the silence."

It's possible I'd never felt so alive as when we took the Seabreacher out the next day. All I know for certain is that diving into the gurgling darkness at 50 miles per hour (and then breaching again, like a dolphin) turned out to be a lot of fun; so much so that we spent the better part of the morning doing just that: diving and breaching, plunging and rising, racing up and down the island (and around its horn, to Pigeon Cay) like damn fools; like college kids on a spring break, which I suppose Amanda was.

That is, until we broke surface and saw the meteor, which was arching across the sky like some orange and black torpedo— like some great, cyclopean flare—painting a trail of smoke and fire as though driven by God Himself; shedding chunks and pieces of itself, like an avalanche. Nor did we slow and try to see where it impacted but rather steered for the shore straight away, beaching the Seabreacher in the shallows near the Big Game Resort and Marina and popping its jetfighter-like hatch, clambering out of it swiftly as the meteor vanished beneath the eastern horizon and the sky exploded: first yellow, or rather a kind of golden amber, then orange, then pink, and finally, after several moments, blue again—although not before the shockwave hit us and blasted us off our feet—straight onto our backs.

"That ... that hit about the same distance away as the first one," I said—after we'd caught our breath and determined neither of us were seriously hurt. *"Holy shit."* I stood and dusted myself off, then peered at the glowing horizon. "Different location, but same basic distance." I must have looked white as a ghost. "Jesus—another P wave. Another primary. And that means—"

"Another *actual wave,"* said Amanda. "Another tsunami—headed this way."

She glared at me and I glared back, both of us knowing full well what that meant. We had about two hours. Two hours before it hit and all hell broke loose. At the max.

She looked at the Seabreacher, which gleamed in the sun, then into its cockpit. "We're going to need that fuel can; the one from the truck. And supplies: food, water, a way to start a fire—"

"Now wait just ... I can't—"

"Do you want to live or not?" she snapped— before placing her hands near the Seabreacher's caudal fin and pushing, trying to turn the boat around. "Because I do. And there's only a quarter tank left in this beast—which isn't enough."

I knelt beside her and helped; shoving as hard as I could, sinking and sliding in the sand—until we'd succeeded in turning the thing around.

"Okay," I said, leaning on the metal, our faces close. "I'll go to the duplex and get the gas—if you want to hit Sue and Joy's and see what you can find. Definitely some bottled water. And a lighter—several of them, if you can. Some toilet paper wouldn't hurt. We'll meet back here in, say—twenty minutes. No later. Okay?"

She looked at me uncertainly, compassionately. "You want to get your picture—don't you? I saw it next your chair. When I—when I left your birthday dinner."

I stared at her for a moment before lowering my gaze, focusing on the sand. "To prove she existed," I said, almost whispering. "To show that—that she was here. She deserves that." I looked out over the ocean. "So do I."

"Well—*go get it, then,* Sebastian. Go get it and get the gas can and get your ass back here. Because I can't do this alone."

And we went—on foot (our vehicles were still parked where we'd found the Seabreacher; on the opposite side of the island): Amanda splitting off for the General Store while I continued on to our duplex, which wasn't far. The hardened twentysomething going one way while I went another—haunted, guilt-ridden, alone.

Understand this: while it certainly *was* a T. rex—or something very much like it—it was not, by any stretch, a monster. It was not, for example, Godzilla (or any other behemoth as depicted in popular movies and books; including, I dare say, *Jurassic Park*). No, this was just an animal, big as an elephant, it's true (but no bigger), and yet, ultimately, no more outlandish than a spotted leopard or a crocodile (at least not since the Flashback); meaning it played well enough with its environment that I hadn't even noticed it—until it was too late.

Too late to get a shot in, anyway—not too late to run; which I did, dropping the gas can and bolting (even as the rex paused to sniff some spoor) before coming to a massive tree (a Caribbean pine, as I recall) and—after jamming the flare gun into my waistband—starting to scale it.

Alas, I'd barely attained the middle limbs when the T. rex arrived—its jaws snapping shut only inches from my shoes and its bellows echoing, furiously. Yet there was little it could do; I'd already climbed beyond its reach (and was climbing higher still). And so we tried to wait each other out, the tyrannosaur and I, as fragments of the meteor began lancing the earth and the doomsday tsunami drew inexorably closer. As the clock ticked mercilessly and Amanda surely fretted and Búi seemed almost to whisper in my ear: *Where have you gone to, my husband, my love, and why have you abandoned me? Is it not obvious—so very, very obvious—where I am? Why, oh why, can't you see?*

At which, inexplicably, I *did* see—something.

A roof.

Just a roof.

Indeed, there wasn't even anything special about it—this roof, other than it was attached to a house I had not seen from the ground—and so had not searched.

I rubbed my eyes and looked at it a second time.

How could we have missed that? Right here, in a wooded section of Alice Town? Right here—not even a block from the Big Game Club Resort and Marina?

I gazed out over the treetops, toward the ocean—and saw it. Saw the wave. Or at least a band of white along the horizon that *looked* like a wave. Was it possible? Búi—I mean? Had she gotten lost—or even injured—and just wandered into the first house she'd come to?

And did I have the time to find out?

And then something just snapped and I was taking out the flare gun and aiming it into the rex's mouth and squeezing the trigger—even as Amanda appeared at the corner of my vision and trained her rifle—after which the rex's maw lit up like a firework and blood jetted from its head (for that's where Amanda had shot it) and the tyrant lizard just collapsed—not threshing about like in the movies, not unfurling its foam latex or CGI tail, but simply slumping forward into the grass like a beached whale until the tip of its snout touched the tree and it was gone. After which I quickly climbed down.

"See?" she said, and chambered a new round. "We make a helluva team." She frowned a little as though she'd just thought of something. "Where's the gas?"

I nodded to where I'd dropped it—about 50 feet away.

"Thank God," she said. She slung the rifle over her shoulder and moved toward it—then paused. "What's wrong?"

I think I just stared at the ground. "I—I spotted something ... up there in the tree. Something we missed. It ... it's in that woodland—right next to the duplex." I lifted my eyes to look at her. "An entire house."

She only gazed at me, saying nothing.

"So, what," she said, finally, "You're just going to mosey back up there and check it out—with the wave practically on top of us? Is that it?"

I nodded, slowly. "Yeah. That's about it." I reached out to touch her but she slapped my hand away. "I'm sorry," I said.

She glared at me as though she might strike me. "Oh, you will be, Sebastian. You will be. Just as soon as that wave arrives." She started to storm off but stopped on a dime. "And for what? Another empty house? Another room full of ghosts? Because there is *nothing here,* Sebastian. *We're it."* Again she started to go, and again she stopped. "What—you think you're the only one who's lost someone? The only one who's lost a wife, or a child, or their parents? Well, I've lost people too—everyone I've ever known. I did! Amanda Everett." Her eyes welled up suddenly and profusely and she swiped at them. "Just because I'm younger than you doesn't make it any easier. And yet we've been given this *chance,* Sebastian. This one chance to face it together; to reboot the world. To literally save it. *To make babies,* for God's sake. And you just want to—you want to—"

And she came at me and we collided, briefly, before embracing—not forcibly (even violently), as had been the case on the jetty, but gently, softly. And then I handed her the flare gun.

"Take it—please," I said. "It—it needs to be with you. And the boat."

She hesitated, staring at the thing, before offering me the rifle, which I declined. Then she took it—the flare gun—decisively, resolutely, and stuffed it beneath her waistband.

"I'm going to wait for you as long as I possibly can, okay? Understand? Five minutes before I leave—I'm gonna to shoot a flare; that'll be your signal to drop anything you're doing and to run, not walk, back to this location." She stared at me with conviction. "Okay?"

"Look, you don't have to—"

"Ah, but I do," she said, and held out her palm. "No less than you have to go check out that house. The flares, please."

I dug them out of my jacket and handed them to her—there were only three. "You shouldn't wait too long. I mean, who knows how big this one will be, or how fast it's moving. But okay. One flare equals five minutes." I stepped back to look at her—to take all of her in. "It—it wasn't just because—"

"Shuttup. Just ... just go do what you got to do. All right?"

She moved to leave but paused.

"Five minutes," she repeated, and then really did go.

What was I feeling as I ascended the stairs to the upper (and last) bedroom of the house? It's impossible to describe; other than to say 'despair' is too weak an expression. No, this was hopelessness and anguish as I could not have imagined—not in my loneliest dreams and nightmares—made worse, no doubt, by my fantasizing along the way; by my sheer, undiluted optimism that each step had somehow brought me closer to my Omega Point, closer to Búi.

But the steps had not been kind—nor had they been quick. And by the time I opened that final door to the final room I had largely succumbed to the inevitable; by which I mean I hardly gave the space a glance—seeing only a jumble of blankets on a four-poster bed and a rickety nightstand crowded with half-emptied bottles of water—before quickly turning to leave.

At which, before I'd even gained the stairs, I froze. Dead in my tracks.

The bottles of water. The plastic containers labelled Aquafina and Dasani—all of them half-full.

My heart thumped against my chest.

"Honey?" I said, in the near perfect silence, "Are you there?"

And then I waited; feeling that even an apparition; even a ghost, a chimera, would be welcome. But there was nothing. Not so much as a creak in the floor. Not so much as a rustling curtain.

But then there *was* something. Just the smallest of voices—indeed, a sound so faint I might have imagined it. Just a small, feint voice which said, simply: "Honey? Is that you?"

And—*Dear God*—I scrambled; rushing back into the room without a moment's hesitation; finding her head exposed outside the tangle of pillows and blankets.

"Honey! Honey!" I knelt beside her at the head of the bed—between her and the open, curtainless window—placing my hands upon her: one on her stomach and one on her head. "Are you all right? Jesus, how have you ..." I looked around the room and saw several empty cans—Dinty Moore Stew and Jack Mackerel, mostly, one of which was entertaining a rat. "Can you move? Can you move, honey? 'Cuz we gotta get you out of here. And I mean, like, *now.*"

I suppose that's when I noticed it; that her eyes were jaundiced and her skin had turned a sickly yellow. And I knew, also, even before I asked her (and she explained it), precisely what had happened: for she had been bitten by something poisonous—a breed of Compy, she said—and had stumbled her way into the house, where she'd been lying, delirious and partially paralyzed, for some three and a half weeks now. Nor was she going anywhere, because the paralysis had presented itself as a kind of full-body muscle spasm, which meant even the slightest movement could cause her excruciating pain.

"But where—where are we now?" she managed—and was interrupted by a coughing jag. "I mean, I remember getting lost; and I remember being bitten, and I remember being stuck in a house for a long, long time. But what I don't remember is how I got *here* ... with you."

I moved to respond but paused, listening. For there was a sound now. A kind of low rumble—which rattled the panes.

I clasped her hand in mine and stroked her forehead, tidied the strands of hair. "We're home, honey. We're back home now. In our stupid little apartment. And—well, it's been a wonderful day, just really nice. We went to Greenbluff—do you remember? To pick cherries. And you picked so many you could hardly carry your buckets, so I had to do it for you—as well as carry my own; but that was all right because I started singing "Beast of Burden" by the Rolling Stones—you know, how I do: badly—and it made you laugh; which to me has always been the best sound in the world. And then we went and got pizza and ate it in the car, and after that, went to my Dad's—to celebrate his 89th birthday. And it was wonderful, just wonderful, with all of us there and the dogs chewing on our shoes and the sky sheltering everything like a big, blue dome; and later, like a dark umbrella."

I heard a *crack!* and a *whoosh* and a *fizzle* and looked out the window; saw the flare rising high like a rocket bound for the Moon: just rising and rising and levelling off—even hovering, briefly, like a UFO—before beginning its glorious fall, its sparkling and brilliant demise, its deep and fatal dive into the Big, Vast Nothing.

She rolled her head on the large, dirty pillow. "Is it—is it the Fourth of July? Are we watching fireworks?"

"Yes, sweetheart, we are." I moved out of her line of sight. *"Look at it, sweetie.* See how it sparks and shines."

"It's so beautiful," she said. "But what—what on earth is that other thing? That sound? It's like—it's like thunder, almost. Or an earthquake."

I moved around to the other side of the bed and got in— nuzzling up against her, holding her so we were perfect spoons. "It's the fireworks, honey, echoing off the buildings. It's nothing to be afraid of. Just a sound. Remember—remember when we went to the Air Show that year, and the sound of the jets scared you so bad that you started hyperventilating? And do you remember what I said to you, that you should just count to 10— and breathe?"

She nodded, her black hair tickling my nose, as the rumbling became a thunder, and then a *roar*.

"Try that now, okay, sweetie? Just count to ten and breathe, all right? Go ahead."

And she started counting, her voice clear and child-like, her accent as strong as ever. "One (inhalation) ... two (inhalation) ... three ... four ..."

"Remember to breathe, honey; do it after every number. I'm right here. *We're all here.* Your children and your parents and my Dad and all your friends. We're in this together—every one of us. And I love you. More than you will ever know. Goodnight, honey."

"Eight ... nine ... ten." There was a moment of silence, or so it seemed. "I love you too, sweetheart."

And then came the waters, surging, crashing, churning, roaring.

And we just breathed.

Deeply.

And yet we did not die—not really. Rather, it felt as though I slept, dreaming ... of the island as seen from the heavens and of floating through a kind of limbo, a kind of purgatory. Of passing over Alice Town and Bailey Town and finally out to sea: where a grain of rice turned out to be the Seabreacher. Of watching that Seabreacher skip and jounce over (and through) the waves like a dolphin—heading toward Miami—and knowing, somehow (for I could see the future now as though it were laid out before me, like a tapestry), that it contained not just Amanda but the dreams and aspirations of all mankind; and that I'd had a part in that.

And, lastly, of being joined by another—so close that our wings brushed—and flying, not like Icarus, not like Daedalus, but purposefully, fearlessly, without regret, into the ancient, seething, fire-pit cauldron of the sun.

MAKE IT A DOUBLE

Warren Benedetto

"What's eating you?" the bartender asked.

He wiped the bar with a rag, lifting napkin holders and bowls of peanuts so he could clean under them. The neon beer signs hanging overhead cast soft-edged splashes of color down onto the reflective wetness of the bar top. He waved at the last group of patrons as they pulled on their jackets and exited the bar. "G'Night!" he called after them. It was almost closing time.

"Fucking Michaelson, that's what," Lewis said. He hunched over a glass of whiskey, watching the ice melt into colorless swirls in the amber liquid. He tapped the base of his ring finger silently against the glass.

Lewis was a short, overweight man with a sullen scowl that carved deep lines from the corners of his mouth down toward where his chin merged with his neck. His crew cut did little to conceal the patchy baldness spreading across his scalp. A roll of skin on the back of his neck prickled with short, stubbly hair. His tie hung loose and crooked around his unbuttoned collar. The weight of his belly pressed against his thighs.

"Him again, huh?" The bartender dried his hands on his apron.

"You bet your ass, him again." Lewis thumped his fist on the bar, causing the pint glasses stacked in front of him to clink together. The bartender reached out and steadied them.

"What is it this time?"

Lewis groaned and massaged his temples as if trying to crush the memory out of existence. He blew out a sour breath, then opened his eyes. "Okay. You know what the real estate market's like these days, right?"

"Pretty bad, right?"

"Really fucking bad." Lewis grabbed a handful of peanuts from the small metal bowl on the bar and swirled them around in his hand. He popped a few in his mouth, then continued as he chewed. "So, there's this couple. Been working on them forever. Months. They've been out to see the unit three, four times already. Can't make up their goddamned minds. But finally, today—finally!—I get them to bite. They say they'll take it."

"Hey, that's great, right? That's good news."

"Fuck yeah, it is. Until—" Lewis laughed bitterly, then took a sip of whiskey from his glass. "Fucking Michaelson."

"What'd he do?"

"I come back to the office. I've got the contract in hand, signed, holding it up like this." Lewis picked up a handful of bar napkins and held them aloft, showing them off to an imaginary crowd. "It's a big deal. Huge. Seven figures. I slam the papers down on my boss' desk." He slapped the napkins down on the bar to illustrate. "I say, 'Sold! Fuck you, pay me.'"

The bartender raised his eyebrows in surprise. "You said that?"

Lewis shrugged. "Yeah, it's all good. We're friends. Besides, there's this contest. He put out a bounty, to try to break the curse, get us motivated. Next person to sell a unit gets an extra one percent commission. Which, on a seven-figure deal..."

"That's a nice little bonus."

"Hell yeah, it is."

"So, what's the problem?"

"What's the problem?" Lewis took another sip of his whiskey, wincing as it went down. He sucked in air through his teeth to cool his burning throat. "Fucking Michaelson, that's the problem."

He tapped the rim of his mostly-empty glass, signaling for a refill. As the bartender poured another shot, Lewis pressed on with the story. "So, I say, 'Fuck you, pay me.' And my boss starts laughing. Everyone else starts laughing too. But, like, *at* me. I get this feeling in my stomach, like, oh no, here we go again. So, I look around. Spot Michaelson. He holds up a contract like this, in one hand." Lewis picked up a handful of napkins and held them up. "Then like this, in the other." He picked up a second pile of napkins in his other hand and held that up too.

"He beat you to it."

"Not once," Lewis said, letting one pile of napkins fall from his hand. "But twice." He let go of the other pile. The napkins fluttered to the floor. "Two units."

"Two units?"

"*Two* goddamned units."

"On the same day?"

"On the *same* goddamned day."

The bartender whistled. "That's some luck."

"Isn't it?" Lewis took a gulp of his whiskey. "Fucking Michaelson."

Lewis stared into his drink with a faraway look, lost in thought. The bartender busied himself with rinsing some stemware that had been soaking in the sink.

Finally, Lewis looked up. His eyes were glassy. "You know what I don't get? Why two?" His voice was thick in his throat.

"Like, I get it, he beat me to it, good for him. He sells one, no problem. But two? Why's he need two? The guy's already got everything." Lewis tapped his ring finger absently against the glass. He sniffed. "Give me that kind of luck for once, you know? Let me get two. One for him, two for me. Is that too much to ask?"

It was a rhetorical question, but the bartender answered anyway. "Not at all."

Lewis tossed back the last swallow of his whiskey, then placed the empty glass back on the bar.

The bartender lifted the bottle of whiskey from the well and tilted it towards Lewis. "One more?"

Lewis placed his hand over the glass and shook his head. "Nah. Close my tab. I'm broke."

"No worries," the bartender said. "I got this one."

Lewis took his hand away from his glass and slid it towards the bartender. "In that case, make it a double."

The bartender laughed. He filled the glass, then flipped a shot glass out from under the bar and filled that too. After dropping the whiskey bottle into the well, he picked up the shot and held it aloft in a toast.

"To Michaelson," he proclaimed. "May whatever luck comes to him, come to you, times two."

"Amen," Lewis said as he clinked his glass with the bartender. "From your mouth to God's ears."

Lewis hung up the phone and angrily scribbled a heavy line through another name on a typed list full of crossed-out names. Then he slammed the pen down on his desk and pushed the list away, disgusted. His chair creaked under his bulk as he leaned back and screwed his fists into his eyes.

After a few seconds, he dropped his hands into his lap and stared at the ceiling. The fire sprinkler overhead peered down at him like a single blood-red eye. He wondered how big of a fire it would take to set the thing off. He pictured the flames licking up the walls, hungrily consuming the bulletin board full of real estate listings, the starburst-shaped SOLD stickers curling and blackening in the heat. He saw the Salesman Of The Month award melting in its cheap acrylic frame, Dan Michaelson's smug, smiling face bubbling and peeling as his photo disintegrated in the fire.

A knocking sound broke Lewis out of his reverie. He sat up and reached for his pen, instinctively trying to look busy.

One of the other salesmen, Duncan, was leaning into his cubicle. "You up for drinks tonight? Michaelson's buying."

A sour bolt of acid shot up the back of Lewis' throat. He swallowed it down. *Fucking Michaelson.*

"Not tonight." Lewis motioned to the list of names on his desk. "Lots of catching up to do."

"Come on, who are you kidding? You're not that busy." Duncan laughed. "If Michaelson's got time, anyone does."

"Funny," Lewis said humorlessly. His lip curled into what he hoped was a smile. How nice for Michaelson that he was able to take a break from being so goddamned perfect for a minute, to lower himself to the rest of their level. Lewis suppressed the urge to flip his desk over. Instead, he said, "That's okay. I'm good."

Duncan looked around furtively, then stepped into Lewis' cubicle and sat on the squat filing cabinet next to Lewis' desk. Lewis unconsciously wheeled his chair backward as Duncan leaned towards him and spoke with a lowered voice.

"Listen, I know it's been hard since Rachel left. I get it. You want to shut down, stay inside, say 'fuck the world.' But that's the worst thing you can do. You need to get out there, have some fun, meet some new people. It's been, what, six months?"

Lewis looked down at his hands. His thumb was tracing lazy arcs across the smooth skin where his wedding ring used to be. "Seven."

"Seven months. That's a long time. And you just made a big sale! You deserve to get out, cut loose a little bit. Put some of that fat commission check to good use."

"That fat commission check didn't even make a dent in what I owe. You know how much a divorce lawyer costs?" Lewis wheeled his chair back up to his desk. He picked up the list of names. "Like I said. I'm busy." He picked up the phone and prepared to dial.

"Okay." Duncan stood up. "You want me to make the hard sell? Here's the hard sell." He grabbed the back of Lewis' chair and pulled him away from the desk. Lewis dropped the phone. It dangled off the edge of the desk, spinning at the end of its cord near the floor. "Get your ass up. Now."

"Duncan, come on—"

"You wanna get wheeled out of here in your chair? Because I'll do it. You're fat, but I'll do it."

Lewis sighed. Duncan wasn't going to give up, and he knew it. The guy was relentless. In sales. In life. In everything. "All right," Lewis said. He slapped his hands on his thighs and reluctantly pressed himself to a standing position. "I'm up. You happy?"

"Good man. Saves me a visit to the chiropractor. Now." He slung his arm around Lewis' shoulders. "You and me and the rest of the guys are going to have some drinks. Michaelson is going to pay, because fuck him. Then we're going to head to the Strip and win some money. And then we're going to meet some ladies—"

"You mean hookers."

Duncan shrugged. "You say potato. Point is, we're gonna have fun, whether you like it or not. Deal?"

"Deal."

Lewis sat at the outside edge of the corner booth, nursing a mostly-empty beer. Duncan was next to him, rambling to the rest of the guys at the table about something-or-other. Lewis wasn't listening. He was too busy watching Michaelson while trying not to stare.

Dan Michaelson was Hollywood handsome with an NFL chin, the best salesman on the team by a long shot. He was charming and popular, the kind of guy who needed a snorkel to keep from drowning in pussy. To make matters worse, he was actually a pretty nice guy. He probably saved puppies from burning buildings on his days off, just for fun.

Lewis hated him.

At the moment, Michaelson was leaning on the bar, hitting on a hot blonde in skin-tight leather pants and a teal crop top. Or was *she* hitting on *him*? It was hard to tell. She was doing that coy thing where she'd laugh, then look down at the floor and push a strand of hair behind her ear, then look up while biting her lower lip. Classic fuck-me move.

The blonde motioned to the bartender, then held up two fingers. The bartender handed her two bottles of beer. She gave one to Michaelson.

Christ Almighty, Lewis thought. ***She's*** *buying* ***him*** *a drink. Unfuckingbelievable.*

Lewis never had a woman offer to buy him a drink in his entire life. Not once. And he never would. If it didn't happen when he was Michaelson's age—when he was younger and thinner and had plenty of hair—it certainly wasn't going to happen now, when he was middle-aged, fat, and balding.

Don't forget broke, his inner voice reminded him. Right, he was broke too.

And yet there was Michaelson, already blessed with every possible advantage in life, having one more thing handed to him. Two, if you counted the blonde. She might as well have a flashing neon *FUCK ME* sign around her neck.

Lewis drained the rest of his beer, then added his bottle to the growing collection of empties in the center of the table. As if on cue, a waitress arrived at the table with a tray of fresh drinks. She was a pretty brunette, short and perky, with crystal blue eyes. Her name tag read *Shelby*.

"Another round, boys," she said. "Courtesy of Captain America over there."

The guys at the table cheered. Michaelson looked over at them and laughed, raising his beer in salute. The waitress distributed the drinks, leaving Lewis for last. She placed a bottle in front of him.

"Thanks," he mumbled, without looking up.

The waitress put a hand on his shoulder and leaned in close to his ear. "You look like you could use another," she whispered. She set a second beer in front of him. Her manicured fingernails gently grazed the side of his neck as she drew her hand away. Goosebumps rushed up his forearms and into his rolled shirtsleeves.

Lewis looked up at her, confused. "What?" He looked down at the pair of beers in front of him, then up at her again. "No, I don't—"

"Shh," she said. "It's on me." She tucked a folded cocktail napkin into Lewis' front shirt pocket, then turned and walked away without another word. Lewis watched her go.

What the hell was that about? he wondered. He reached into his pocket and unfolded the napkin. Written on it in pink ballpoint pen were the words, "Find me after." It was signed, "Shelby." The tail of the "y" looped into a tiny heart at the end.

Lewis looked up again, searching the bar for the waitress, but she was gone.

Lewis slid out of the booth. His co-workers piled out after him. They were all wasted. Duncan fake-punched Lewis in the stomach as he stood. Lewis flinched. Duncan laughed. "Gotcha," he slurred.

"You know it," Lewis said, distractedly. He scanned the crowd, looking for the waitress who had slipped him the napkin.

"Let's go win some money," Duncan said. "Casino. Go, go, go." He nudged Lewis towards the exit.

"We got room for one more?" a syrupy voice said from behind. "Amber says she's feeling lucky."

Lewis looked over his shoulder. It was Michaelson. He towered over Lewis by a good six inches, maybe seven. More, if you counted his perfectly-coiffed hair. It was thick and lustrous, effortlessly perfect, as if every strand was self-aware and knew exactly where it should be. Even the strands that were out of place looked like they had been carefully positioned there by God himself.

The blonde from the bar was tucked neatly under Michaelson's arm. Her fingers were laced in his, her bright red nails glistening like liquid under the overhead lights. Her other hand was tucked into the back pocket of his jeans.

"Hell yeah, we do," Duncan said. He punched Michaelson in the arm.

Michaelson laughed. Amber did too. Lewis felt a fresh surge of disgust coursing through his veins. He hadn't been with a woman since his wife left. But Michaelson? He could have anyone he wanted, any time he wanted. He didn't even have to try. They flew at him from all directions, like moths to a streetlamp. He probably had to swat them away with a tennis racket.

Michaelson thumped Lewis on the back. "How you doin', my man?" he asked jovially. "Having fun yet?" Lewis opened his mouth to respond, but Michaelson didn't wait for an answer. Instead, he leaned close to Amber and said something into her ear, something Lewis couldn't hear. She laughed.

Bitter bile bubbled up in the back of Lewis' throat, burning his esophagus. They were talking about him. He knew it. And whatever they were saying, it probably wasn't nice. Guys like Michaelson didn't say nice things to pretty girls about guys like him. Lewis had dealt with Michaelson's type his whole life. Super friendly on the surface, until they decide you're inferior. Then they're shoving you in a locker, or stealing your clothes while you're in the shower, or pantsing you in front of the whole gym class.

"Let's go! Train's leaving!" Duncan yelled.

Lewis stepped aside. "You know what? I'm gonna hit the head real quick. I'll catch up with you."

Lewis waited until the group was gone, then pulled the waitress' note out of his shirt pocket. He unfolded it covertly, down by his hip, and read it again. He wanted to reassure himself that he hadn't misread it. That it was real. It was. The words were clear and unambiguous: "Find me after."

He refolded the note, then headed to the end of the bar. His pulse was racing. He waved to the bartender. "Shelby?" he shouted over the music. The bartender's hands were full carrying a rack of clean glasses. He thrust his chin, signaling for Lewis to turn around. He did. Shelby was behind him. She had traded her waitress uniform for civilian clothes: low-waisted jeans and a tight white t-shirt that contrasted with her tanned skin. Her dark hair was gathered into two braids, one on each side of her head.

"Want some company?" she asked with a coy smile.

"Um, sure." Lewis' mouth suddenly felt like it was full of dry cotton, like his tongue was wearing a sweater. He had no idea what was happening, no frame of reference for a random woman in a bar who was ... what? Flirting with him? Is that what she was doing? Sure seemed like it.

"Sweet!" Shelby turned and cupped her hands around her mouth. "Crystal!" she shouted. She waved and beckoned with a "come here" gesture.

Another girl emerged from the crowd. She seemed to be about Shelby's age—mid-twenties, Lewis thought—and was dressed similarly, in tight jeans and a white halter top. Her auburn hair was pulled into a ponytail at the back of her head.

Shelby took Crystal's hand, then turned back to Lewis.

"All right, let's go."

"You want to do the honors?" Lewis asked. He was sitting on a plush velvet stool in front of a towering slot machine with the words *MONEY MADNESS* emblazoned on the front. Shelby was sitting on his knee, sipping a bright green drink through a skinny straw. Crystal stood behind him, leaning in close. He could feel her breasts pressed against his back. It felt nice.

"Come on, big money!" Shelby called out. She slammed her palm down on the SPIN button. A too-loud jingle blared from the machine's speakers, adding to the cacophony of the casino floor. Crystal whooped enthusiastically, then laughed. Lewis laughed too. He was having fun.

The first wheel stopped on cherries.

The second wheel stopped. Cherries again.

"Let's go let's go let's go!" Shelby cheered. She crossed her fingers and closed her eyes.

The third wheel stopped.

Lemon.

Shelby opened her eyes and let out a groan of disappointment. Crystal did too. Shelby pouted out her lower lip. "I suck at this," she whined. "I'm sorry."

"Don't worry about it," Lewis said. "It's fine."

"But we lost all your money," Crystal said.

Sure enough, the digital *Balance* readout on the machine read $00.00.

"It's not 'all my money,'" Lewis said. He patted her thigh. "Here. Get up." Shelby climbed off Lewis' knee and stepped out of the way as he stood. "You two stay here. I'll hit the ATM."

"You sure?" Shelby asked.

"Sure, I'm sure," Lewis said with easy confidence.

Shelby threw her arms around Lewis' neck and gave him a peck on the cheek. "You're the best," she said.

Lewis blushed. "Be right back."

He walked down the long aisle of slot machines, then looked back towards Shelby and Crystal. They were both seated on the velvet stool, sharing it half-and-half, looking at their phones and waiting for him to return.

"Shit, shit, shit," he said under his breath. He had lost way more than he planned—way more than he could afford—first at the blackjack table, then at poker, and now at the slots. He rarely gambled, and this was why: he was really bad at it. In fact, he had never won much of anything, ever. He knew he should call it a night and cut his losses, but the truth was, he didn't want to. He was having more fun than he'd had in a long, long time. It was worth it.

He got to the ATM, inserted his card, and typed in his PIN. His finger hovered over the Withdrawal button for a moment, before course-correcting to hit the Check Balance button instead. The machine processed the request, then displayed his current balance: $-370.00.

Ouch.

Suddenly, a loud cheer rose from the bank of slot machines nearby. A chorus of bells and chimes started ringing. More voices joined in the cheering. People began to applaud. Lewis froze. His stomach dropped. He didn't even need to see, to know who it was. *Fucking Michaelson.* It had to be.

Lewis turned around. Sure enough, Michaelson was standing in front of a slot machine that had JACKPOT flashing across the screen in a dozen different fonts and colors. A red police light on top of the machine was spinning gleefully. Michaelson's fists were thrust towards the ceiling in celebration. Amber, the blonde from the bar, gave him a two-handed high five, then wrapped her arms around his neck. Her hands entwined in his hair as she kissed him deeply. Meanwhile, the digits on the jackpot counter grew and grew, eventually topping out at $10,000.

Lewis pivoted back to the ATM, away from Michaelson's celebration. He felt like he was going to throw up. How could one guy be so blessed, while another—himself, specifically— could be so cursed? Was God playing favorites? Is that what it was? Or was it that certain advantages conferred other advantages which conferred still more advantages, and so on, until life was throwing money and pussy at you all day and night? Lewis wondered what his life would have been like if he had been born taller, or thinner, or smarter. Maybe he'd be the one winning all the time. Maybe his bank account would be a positive number. Maybe Rachel wouldn't have left him for—

"Hey, everything okay?" a sweet voice asked. A hand touched his arm. Lewis turned. Shelby and Crystal were behind him. "You disappeared," Shelby said.

"We thought you ditched us," Crystal added with a wink.

"Yeah, no, I'm fine," Lewis said. "Just got distracted by my friend over there." He nodded his head towards Michaelson.

"Lucky guy," Shelby said.

"Yeah. Sure is." His smile felt like a mouthful of porcelain tiles that might shatter at any moment. "Lemme just ..." He indicated the ATM. Shelby got the hint.

"Oh, yeah. Do what you've gotta do. We'll be over here."

The girls walked away, leaving Lewis alone. He pulled out his wallet, replaced his ATM card, and withdrew a Visa card instead. He inserted it into the ATM, then selected the Cash Advance option. His finger lingered over the number pad as he debated how much to withdraw. *Fuck it.* He punched in 500.00 and hit Enter. The machine dispensed a pile of twenty-dollar bills. Lewis folded them into a thick wad and shoved them into his front pocket. He walked back over to where Shelby and Crystal were waiting. "All right, where to?"

"Right here." Shelby pointed to the slot machine she was standing next to. "I have a good feeling about this one."

The graphic on the front of the machine featured a man in a tuxedo leaning against the side of a limousine. Clinging to each of his arms was a gorgeous woman. One was a pouting Marilyn Monroe type in a tight pink *Gentlemen Prefer Blondes* gown. The other was a rip-off of *Breakfast At Tiffany's* era Audrey Hepburn, complete with sunglasses, cigarette holder, and diamond-studded crown. The man's eyebrow was arched as if to say, "Ain't this the life?" Behind him, triple spotlights illuminated hilltop letters that mimicked the Hollywood sign. They spelled out the name of the machine: DOUBLE LUCKY.

Double rip-off if more like it, Lewis thought. He wasn't going to say that to Shelby though. No point in spoiling a good thing. Instead, he pulled out the bundle of bills from the ATM, peeled off a fresh twenty, and inserted it into the machine. The digital *Balance* readout updated to read $20.00. "Okay. Who's turn is it?"

"Yours," Shelby replied. She gave Lewis a peck on the cheek. In response to his surprised expression, she said, "For good luck."

Crystal stepped closer and placed a kiss on Lewis' other cheek. "Make it a double."

From your mouth to God's ears, Lewis thought. Then he pressed the SPIN button. A rousing big band tune blasted from the machine. The wheels accelerated into a blur.

The first wheel stopped. Double Jackpot.

The second wheel stopped. Double Jackpot again.

"Come on, come on!" Shelby squealed. Crystal bounced and clapped excitedly. Lewis' heart was beating like a boxer's speed bag.

The third wheel kept spinning.

And spinning.

Finally, it stopped.

Double Jackpot.

Pandemonium. Shelby and Crystal started screaming and jumping up and down in celebration. Every light on the slot machine began to flash. The speakers blared a celebratory big band tune. A pair of police sirens began to wail. An artificial *ching-ching-ching* sound effect blasted from all directions, emulating the sound of a slot machine paying out a fuck-ton of quarters. The hilltop letters flashed on and off in an alternating pattern: DOUBLE! LUCKY! DOUBLE! LUCKY! DOUBLE! LUCKY!

"You won!" Shelby threw her arms around Lewis' shoulders. Crystal embraced him too. Lewis just stared dumbly at the screen.

"I won?" he asked, in a distant voice. His face was blank, unbelieving.

"Yes, you won!" Crystal said. "Look!"

She pointed at the digital jackpot counter as the numbers grew and grew: $10,000 ... $15,000 ... $20,000. That's where they stopped. Double jackpot.

Twice what Michaelson had just won.

For a brief moment, the words of the bartender from last night drifted through Lewis' mind like a wisp of smoke. *May whatever luck comes to him, come to you, times two.* Then it was gone.

"I won," Lewis said again, more sure this time. Then, with growing enthusiasm: "I won!" A burst of delirious laughter escaped from his lips. It sounded something like happiness. Felt a little like it too.

The crowd that had previously surrounded Michaelson surged towards Lewis. They clapped and cheered and high-fived each other. Duncan pushed through the crowd and yelled in Lewis' face. *"Woooooo!"* He grabbed Lewis' shoulders and shook him back and forth. Lewis' head bobbed on his neck. "Yes, baby, yes!" Duncan pounded a fist on Lewis' chest. "That's what I'm talking about!" Then he threw an arm around Lewis' shoulder and hollered to the crowd. "This is my man, right here!" The crowd cheered even louder. He put Lewis in a friendly headlock and said into his ear, "There's your 'Fuck you, pay me.' Am I right?"

Lewis ran his hand over his stubbly hair, wiping away a slick of perspiration that had appeared on his scalp. He felt a swell of emotion rising in his chest. The muscles in his face felt taut. He exhaled a shuddering breath. It felt good to win for once; it had been so long. He made a mental note to thank Duncan for forcing him to go out. Duncan was right: he needed it.

Lewis scanned the crowd. He wanted Michaelson to see him, to know that he could be a winner too. That not everything in life always went to the quarterback or the class president. That the guy from the math club could get the girl too. *Or girls,* Lewis thought as he looked at Shelby and Crystal. *Plural.*

Unfortunately, Michaelson wasn't in the crowd. Instead, Lewis spotted him across the casino lobby, walking away with his arm around Amber's waist. She clutched his tanned, muscled bicep, her head leaning against his shoulder.

Lewis felt a sudden panic. Michaelson wasn't even looking. He wasn't going to see. The whole moment would be lost. It would all be for nothing.

"Hey!" Lewis called over the din. "Hey, Michaelson!"

Michaelson stopped. He looked around, vaguely aware that someone had called his name.

Lewis waved his arms. "Over here!"

Michaelson spotted Lewis. He crinkled his brow and gave a little nod as if to say, "What's up?"

"Check it out!" Lewis shouted. "I won! Double jackpot!"

Michaelson's lips said, "Wow." He gave Lewis a thumbs up. Then he pointed at the top of Amber's head, then towards the elevators. He mouthed, "I'm gonna go."

Lewis made an OK sign, then watched as Michaelson escorted Amber into the elevator.

As the doors slid shut, Lewis was suddenly filled with an almost unbearable sense of self-loathing. So he won? So what? Winning didn't take any skill. It was luck, pure and simple. Some random number generator in a computer somewhere spit out the right combination, and he was the dumb fuck who was lucky enough to be sitting in front of the machine when it happened. Tomorrow, he'd go right back to being Ron Lewis, Loser For Life. It didn't matter how much money he won. He was worthless.

That's not true, another voice in his head countered. What about Shelby? And Crystal? That wasn't just dumb luck. No computer made Shelby slip him that note. She and Crystal could have bailed hours ago, but they didn't. That had to mean something.

It had to.

"You'll still be here when I get out?" Lewis asked.

To claim his winnings, he had to go with a casino manager to fill out some paperwork in an office somewhere. The casino was authorized to pay out up to $10,000 in cash, which is why Michaelson was able to just walk away with his prize. But the size of Lewis' jackpot meant the casino had to cut him a check instead. And that would take time.

Shelby looked at Crystal. Crystal shrugged and nodded. "Fine with me."

Shelby replied, "Sure. We've got nowhere else to be. Where should we meet you?"

Lewis looked around for a good meeting spot. There was a piano lounge on the other side of the lobby. "How about in there?"

"We'll be there," Shelby said.

"Promise?"

"Promise."

Lewis watched them glide across the lobby and disappear into the lounge. *God, they're beautiful,* he thought. Then he walked over to the casino manager waiting nearby.

"They're with you?" the manager asked.

"Yep."

"Both of them?"

"Yep."

"Nice," the manager said, with a knowing nod and a sly smile. "Very nice."

Lewis felt a little bump of something unfamiliar jolt through his bloodstream. He wasn't used to another guy reacting to him with ... what, exactly? Was it envy? Or at least admiration? Something like that. It was probably just a tiny, coffee-creamer-sized serving of how Michaelson felt all the time, but it was nice.

I could get used to this, Lewis thought.

He hustled to the casino office and rushed through the paperwork as quickly as he could, trying desperately to hang onto the rapidly evaporating contrails of happiness left behind from his win. His leg jittered and bounced while he waited for his check to be cut. He looked at his watch so many times that his shoulder started to ache. It took almost an hour. It felt like forever.

By the time he was done, Lewis' thin veneer of confidence had worn off, leaving a dull, rusted panic in its place. He took the check without even looking at it, stuffed it in his pocket, then tore out of the casino office and made a beeline for the piano lounge.

The lounge was a tiny space with a short, curved bar and a few cocktail tables arranged around a large piano. It was dimly lit with blue light that spilled out from under the edge of the bar.

Aside from the bartender, the place was empty.

Lewis' stomach fell off a cliff, turning over and over as it plunged into darkness. The girls had ditched him. They had promised to stay, and they were gone. Just like his wife, like his dad, like everyone who fucking mattered in his life. And yet he kept falling for it, over and over, every goddamned time. He felt so stupid.

"Hey!" The bartender waved his towel to get Lewis' attention. "You Lewis?"

Lewis pointed at his chest. "Me? Yeah. I'm Lewis."

"They'll be right back. They went to the bathroom."

Lewis' stomach bounced off the floor and up into his throat. He laughed a little, relieved. "Okay, great. Thought I lost 'em."

He took a seat at one of the cocktail tables. A minute later, Shelby and Crystal returned. They saw him and walked over to where he sat.

"Hey! Did the bartender...?" Shelby started.

"Yeah, he told me."

"Okay, good." She pulled out a chair and sat down. Crystal did too. "We didn't want you to think we bailed."

"No, of course not," Lewis lied. "I would never think that."

"So, now what?" Shelby asked. She looked at Crystal.

"Up to you," Crystal said.

Lewis rubbed his palms back and forth along the tops of his thighs. His hands were freezing, but sweating. He was more nervous than he had ever been about anything in his life.

He had an idea. It came to him while he was waiting in the casino office, and he spent the rest of the time trying to decide what to do about it. It was something he had never thought about before—never even considered as a possibility for someone like him—but what the hell ... he was feeling lucky. Maybe tonight would be the night.

"Yeah, so I was thinking ..." His voice seemed to be disconnected from his brain. It was like he was floating outside his body, watching himself talk. He couldn't believe what he was saying. "The casino comped me a room for the night, so I thought maybe you two might want to come up and hang out or something."

Shelby and Crystal exchanged glances. Shelby shifted uncomfortably in her chair. "Um, I don't know if that's such a good idea."

Lewis' stomach tightened. He felt the overwhelming urge to retreat, to just curl up into a ball and roll out of the bar in shame. But then he pictured Michaelson, so confident, heading to the elevators with Amber—a girl he had met only hours before—wrapped around his finger. Michaelson wouldn't give up that easily, would he? Fuck no, he wouldn't.

"Why not?" Lewis asked. "We've been having a good time, right? Let's keep it going."

"Yeah, we have, but ..." Shelby struggled to find the right words. "But we're not, like ..." She looked at Crystal with a *help me* expression.

"It's just a no, okay?" Crystal said. She started to stand, looking at Shelby with a pointed glare. "We should go."

"Yeah." Shelby stood up too. She slung her purse over her shoulder. "Yeah, it's getting late." She extended her hand to Lewis. "It was nice meeting you though."

Lewis sat back in his chair and folded his arms over his chest. "So that's it, then?" he said, looking from Shelby to Crystal and back to Shelby. Shelby awkwardly lowered her hand.

Crystal spoke up. "Look, your friend didn't say anything about—" Shelby bumped Crystal with her elbow. Crystal rolled her eyes. "Can we just go?" she said to Shelby. "It's enough already."

Lewis sat up straight in his chair. "Friend? What friend?"

"Nothing," Shelby said. "Don't listen to her."

"No, tell me. What friend? What did he say? Was it Duncan?" Lewis' heart was trying to kick its way out of his rib cage. His face felt hot. His eyes burned. What did Duncan tell her? And why?

"He paid us, alright?" Crystal tugged Shelby's arm. "I told you this guy's a creep. Let's go."

Shelby ignored Crystal. "I'm sorry," Shelby said to Lewis. "I'm just a waitress. I'm not a ... you know. I don't do those kinds of things. Not for money. And Crystal's just my friend. I asked her to come." Lewis was staring past her, into space. She tried to make eye contact with him. "I really did have a nice time though."

"So, what *do* you do for money?" Lewis asked coldly. His eyes narrowed and connected with Shelby's. She took a step backward as if pushed by an unseen hand. The expression on her face turned from one of sympathy to one of fear. *Good,* Lewis thought.

"Hey, it's not our fault you can't get girls on your own," Crystal sneered.

"Crystal!" Shelby spun at her, mortified. She pointed out of the lounge, at the lobby. "Wait out there, please," she snapped. "You're not helping."

"But—"

"Go!"

Crystal snatched her jacket off the back of the chair and stormed away. "This is so stupid."

Shelby watched her friend leave, then turned back to Lewis. His elbows were on the cocktail table. His face was in his hands.

"Hey, listen," Shelby said. "I'm sorry, okay? That was out of line."

"Who paid you?" Lewis asked quietly. His voice was muffled by his hands. He dragged his hands down his face. They fell in his lap, limp. He tilted his head back, his face towards the ceiling. His eyes were closed. "Was it Duncan?"

"Duncan?" Shelby's eyes rolled upwards, as she tried to remember the name. "No, it was ... your friend, you know, the guy who— Captain America, who bought your drinks. Michael-something."

Lewis opened his eyes. He couldn't believe what he was hearing. *Fucking Michaelson?!* That motherfucker. He tried to speak, but his voice was just a whisper. "Michaelson," he said.

"Yeah, that's it. He said he felt bad. Something about a bonus you didn't get? He wanted you to have a good time, asked if we would help. Said you've had a tough run of it lately, that you deserved some fun." She tried to catch Lewis' eyes again. "He was trying to help you."

Lewis leaned forward and glared at Shelby. His eyes looked like two black marbles, cold and lifeless. His voice was a low growl. "How much did he pay you?"

Shelby looked at the floor. Her cheeks were damp. "A thousand."

Lewis laughed bitterly. "A thousand," he repeated.

"Each," Shelby finished.

Lewis looked down at his hands. They were clenched into fists. His knuckles were white. "Get out."

Shelby wiped her eyes with the heel of her hands, smearing her makeup. "I'm sorry. I didn't mean to—"

"Get! Out!" Lewis yelled. He pounded both fists down on the cocktail table. The heavy mirrored tabletop shattered under the blow, disintegrating into a shower of broken glass. Shelby recoiled, then ran from the piano lounge. She didn't look back.

Lewis held his hands up in front of his face. Shards of glass were embedded in his flesh. Dark rivers of blood ran down his wrists and dripped onto the floor. He felt no pain, only rage. He was angry at the girls for deceiving him, for making him think they were there for him, instead of the money. He was angry at himself for falling for it. And he was angry at Michaelson for, well, everything.

A blur of motion drew Lewis' attention toward the bar. The bartender had picked up a phone on the wall. He kept one eye on Lewis as he started to dial. Lewis saw him. "Hey!" he shouted. He jumped up, sending the chair tumbling backward. He pushed the remains of the broken table out of his way. It crashed to the floor. Lewis' shoes crunched on the broken glass. He strode towards the bar, plunging one of his bloodied hands deep into his pocket as he went.

The bartender dropped the phone and raised his hands in front of his chest, palms out. "Please, don't—"

Lewis pulled out the thick wad of twenties he had withdrawn from the ATM earlier. He flung them at the bartender. The bartender flinched, shielding his face with his hands. A spray of blood droplets flew through the air with the money, peppering the bartender's white shirt as the cash hit him in the chest and dropped to the floor.

When the bartender lowered his hands away from his face, Lewis was gone.

Lewis sat in his car with the engine running. His headlights were off. The roof of the casino parking garage was dotted with pools of light surrounded by wide spans of inky darkness. Lewis' car was in the shadows. His was one of only two vehicles remaining on the roof level. The other was a Tesla.

Michaelson's Tesla.

It was parked at the opposite end of the parking garage, near a large assembly of massive industrial fans that provided ventilation for the casino. The roar of the fans was loud, loud enough for Lewis to hear them even with his windows closed. They made a droning hum that seemed to pulse in time with his heartbeat.

Lewis' hands were on the steering wheel. His breathing was calm. Steady. The blood on his forearms had dried into twisted brown smears. Tiny shards of glass still poked from his skin. He ignored them. His eyes were fixed on a single spot across the garage: a blue metal door, under a glowing green sign that read *EXIT.*

Lewis wasn't sure how long he had been sitting there. It seemed like hours. The sky to the east was a filthy, grayish-yellow color that reminded Lewis of his father's tobacco-stained teeth. It was the beginnings of a sunrise, he supposed. He'd be expected to be in the office in a few short hours. He didn't care. He would never be going to work again.

The blue metal door opened. Lewis sat forward in his seat, suddenly alert. A figure was silhouetted in the doorway, backlit against the light from the stairwell. Lewis couldn't tell who it was. But then he heard the *chirp-chirp* of a car alarm being deactivated. The tail lights on Michaelson's Tesla blinked twice.

It was him.

Lewis watched as Michaelson strolled towards the Tesla, spinning the key fob around his index finger as he walked. His stride was casual, confident, the walk of a man on an unbroken path, whose perfect life was unfolding perfectly before him, every day proceeding exactly as planned. Everything was right for him. Everything worked to his advantage. There was nothing out of place. Nothing incomplete. No desire unfulfilled. Every pitch was a strike. Every at-bat, a home run. Every game a perfect game. A life unspoiled by defeat, or disappointment, or loss.

Until now.

As Michaelson passed in front of Lewis' car, Lewis flipped on his high beams.

Michaelson froze, suddenly blinded by the searing light. He threw up his forearm in front of his face to shield his eyes from the glare. His expression was confused, uncomprehending.

Lewis slammed his foot down on the gas pedal, smashing it to the floor. His tires squealed. Black smoke poured out from under his rear bumper. The car lurched forward, accelerating towards Michaelson.

Michaelson's reaction was delayed. Maybe he was still buzzed from a long night of drinking, or maybe his brain just couldn't quite fathom what was happening. By the time his legs started moving, Lewis' car was already closing in on him.

Michaelson ran.

He sprinted straight at first. Then he zigzagged to the left, then to the right. Lewis tracked his every move, keeping him dead center between his headlights. Michaelson threw a look over his shoulder. His face was a mask of abject terror. He was going to die, and he knew it.

Just as Lewis' car was upon him, Michaelson dove to his right. The car hit him while he was airborne, throwing him up over the hood. His shoulder collided with the windshield, shattering it into a spiderweb of fractured glass. The impact sent him over the roof, his body cartwheeling sideways into the bank of industrial fans. A horrible grinding sound echoed through the parking garage as his unconscious body smashed through the fans' protective grating and into the powerful blades inside.

Lewis' car continued straight, heading for the edge of the parking garage roof.

He never slowed down.

Lewis was awake.

There hadn't been any feeling of waking up or coming to. No gradual transition from unconscious to conscious. It was like someone had just flipped a switch. There was nothing, and then there was something. He realized he could hear noises: beeps and hisses and the gentle drone of an air conditioner or a fan. But he couldn't see anything. Everything was black.

He heard a voice. A man's voice. It was muffled and distorted, like it was being played on toy speakers from a vinyl record that had warped in the heat. He didn't recognize the voice, but he understood the words.

"Mr. Lewis? Can you hear me?"

Lewis tried to speak, but his throat felt like he had swallowed a bale of barbed wire. He suddenly realized that he was choking. Something seemed to be in his throat, gagging him. He panicked, trying to lift his hand to pull out whatever it was, so he could breathe. But he couldn't move. As hard as he tried, he couldn't lift his arms. Either of them. He didn't understand. What was happening? Was he tied down? Or...

With dawning horror, Lewis tried to move his legs. He couldn't feel them either. *Oh my God,* Lewis thought. *I'm paralyzed.* He tried to sit up, but a strong pair of hands pressed on his shoulders, holding him down.

"Hey, now. Take it easy. Just relax," a different voice said, closer to his face. This one belonged to a woman. Its tone was firm but kind.

Who are you? Lewis wanted to scream. *Where am I?*

He lifted his head and tried to sit up again, but the hands held him down. Then he realized: he could *feel* the hands on his shoulders. If he was paralyzed, he wouldn't be able to feel them touching him, right? Lewis relaxed. He settled back into the mattress. Maybe he wasn't paralyzed after all.

As he stopped struggling, the hands released their pressure on his shoulders.

The man's voice spoke again. "Mr. Lewis, I'm Doctor Grace. If you can hear me, can you nod?"

Lewis nodded.

"Great," the doctor said. "Do you know where you are?"

Lewis shook his head. "No," he croaked. His throat felt like it was full of broken glass.

"Okay. You're in Our Lady of Mercy hospital. We just removed a tube from your throat, so it's best if you don't try to talk just yet. It's going to be pretty raw for a while."

Lewis nodded again. He swallowed, then winced. It hurt like hell.

"Do you remember anything about what happened?"

Lewis shook his head again. But as soon as he did, a series of memories flickered across his mind like still frames from an old-time flipbook. The casino. The girls. The double jackpot. The cocktail table, shattered. The car. Michaelson.

Fucking Michaelson.

Now a different voice spoke. Another man. One he recognized.

"Hey, Lewis. It's Mike Duncan, from work. You remember me?"

Lewis nodded. He remembered Duncan. He sat in the next cubicle over, at the office.

"I just stopped by to see how you were doing, and ... well, I guess I got lucky. The doctor says this is the first time you've been awake since the accident."

The accident? Lewis thought. So they thought it was an accident. That was good.

"Water," Lewis whispered.

The woman's voice spoke. Maybe a nurse? "It's too soon to give you water, but I can get you some ice if you'd like."

Lewis nodded. "Please."

"Coming right up." He heard the woman walking away, her footsteps muted on the tile floor.

"I'll give you a few minutes with your friend," the doctor said.

"Thanks, Doctor," Duncan responded. Heavier footsteps. Then a door closed and latched with a *click.*

"Can you talk?" Duncan asked.

Lewis opened his jaw and moved his tongue around. It felt foreign to him, like a piece of raw meat in his mouth. He swallowed again. Flames tore at his esophagus. "Hey," he managed to whisper. His voice sounded like a handful of crinkling straw. "What happened?"

"Oh, man," Duncan said. His voice was shaky. "Well ... there was an accident. But you're okay. You made it through."

"Michaelson," Lewis croaked.

"He made it too," Duncan said. "He—" His voice cut out, choked by a sob. "I'm sorry. I just ... Man, this is so fucked up."

"He's okay?" Lewis asked.

Duncan coughed out a mortified laugh, in spite of himself. "Not really. He got chewed up pretty bad. Lost an arm. A leg. An eye. His whole right side is just ... it's bad. He barely made it. And he's not out of the woods yet. Has a long way to go. Years, they said."

Lewis felt a wave of familiar anger boiling inside him. *Of course, Michaelson survived,* Lewis thought with bitter sarcasm. *Of course, he did.*

Lewis was such a loser that he couldn't even murder someone without fucking it up.

But then a different thought occurred to him. Dying was easy. Almost *too* easy. But surviving? Surviving was a bitch. Surviving meant Michaelson would have to live the rest of his life handicapped, disfigured, partially blind, while the whole time knowing what he used to be. What he had lost. What he could never be again. The more Lewis thought about it, the better the whole thing sounded.

Then Duncan spoke again, interrupting Lewis' internal monologue. "Rachel came to see you."

The words hit Lewis head-on, crushing him like a car in one of those crash tests where someone drives a Hyundai into a brick wall. His heart seemed to stop for a second, suspended in mid-air, before tripping over itself to regain its rhythm.

Rachel? *His* Rachel? He felt a sob rising in his throat. The very idea that she was there for him, that she came back after everything that had happened between them, after everything he had said, everything he had done ... it was overwhelming.

Maybe she still loved him.

Maybe there was still a chance for them after all.

"She's here?" Lewis asked, his voice wavering on the edge of tears. Duncan was silent. Lewis asked again, more clearly this time. "Duncan? Is she here?"

"No," he said quietly. "Not today. She came when she heard what happened but, she, uh ... she left. She didn't want to see you like this."

"Like what?"

There was another long silence. Finally, Duncan spoke. "Maybe I should get the doctor." Lewis heard a chair creak as Duncan stood.

"Duncan, wait. Like what?" Lewis asked again. "What's happening? Am I paralyzed?"

Duncan didn't answer. Lewis heard the door open, followed by the soft footsteps of the nurse's sneakers and the louder *clacks* of the doctor's loafers.

Duncan put his hand on Lewis' shoulder. "I'm gonna run. It was good to see you. Stay strong, brother."

Lewis tried to reach up and pat Duncan's hand, but he still couldn't move his arm. He settled for a nod. "Thanks for coming, Mike."

Duncan's footsteps receded out of the room. Then Lewis felt the cold wetness of ice on his lips.

"Here you go," the nurse said softly. "Some ice for you." Lewis opened his mouth. The nurse spooned a small portion of soft, tasteless ice chips into his mouth. They dissolved on his tongue, sending a trickle of freezing water down his shredded throat. It felt good.

"Thanks," he whispered.

Lewis heard the sound of a wheeled stool being rolled closer. It squeaked as the doctor sat. "Mr. Lewis, we need to talk—"

"Am I paralyzed?" Lewis asked.

"No," the doctor confirmed. "You're not paralyzed. Luckily, the damage from the crash didn't affect your spine. You did have a severe concussion, and some pretty serious swelling in your brain, but we were able to manage that effectively. There should be no permanent brain damage."

Lewis felt a wave of relief. No permanent damage. *Good, good.*

The doctor continued. "The accident was very serious, but between the airbags, the seat belt, and the other safety features, you made it out relatively unscathed, considering." Lewis heard paper turning, as if the doctor was flipping through his chart. "Concussion, severe contusions and lacerations, stitches and staples in your scalp, a few broken ribs, broken tibias, left and right ... I know this sounds like a lot, but given the severity of the accident, it's incredible that you survived it at all. You're a very lucky man, Mr. Lewis." He heard the doctor close his file. "Do you remember anything about what happened?"

"Not much." Lewis' thoughts turned inwards as he tried to remember. The longer he was awake, the more his memory started to fill in, like a roll of film developing in a chemical bath. There was still a thin gauze over the whole night, a milky cataract that obscured some of the details, but he began to remember more distinctly the events that preceded the crash. The waitress giving him the extra beer. The note in his pocket. Her and her friend coming with him to the casino. Winning the double jackpot.

Then, the piano lounge.

The embarrassment.

The betrayal.

Michaelson had paid them. He thought Lewis was so pathetic that the only way that a girl would hang out with him was if she was paid to do it.

Fucking Michaelson, he thought for the thousandth time.

"... we did everything we could, but—"

Lewis realized that the doctor was still talking. He hadn't been listening. All of his mental energy had gone to piecing together the memories of that night.

"Sorry, can you repeat that?" Lewis said. "I was ... it's hard to focus ..."

"Yes, of course," the doctor said. "I understand this is a lot to process. I can come back later when you're feeling stronger—"

"No, no, it's all right. Just say that again? Before 'we did everything we could' ...?"

"Okay." The doctor took a deep breath and exhaled. "I was saying that you were lucky to survive the accident. You and Mr. Michaelson both: very, very lucky. But after ..." The doctor's voice wavered as if he was on the edge of tears. "Mr. Lewis, I am so sorry. We did everything—" There was a click in his throat as he swallowed a hitching breath. "We did everything we could. But the infection was just too aggressive. It was resistant to antibiotics, to every intervention we tried."

A heavy veil of dread draped over Lewis like a lead blanket. He could feel it pressing on his chest, compressing his lungs, collapsing his rib cage. Terror tightened around his throat like a noose, threatening to strangle him.

"The infection was pervasive, and ... and extensive," the doctor continued. "We fought it with everything we had. But in the end, we had no choice but to ..." The doctor took another shaky breath. "But to amputate."

Amputate. The word shot through Lewis' head like a hollow-point bullet, shredding his mind into jagged ribbons of horror as it exploded through his skull.

"My arms," he managed to say.

"Yes," the doctor replied. "I'm sorry. Your arms. And your legs. And ... and your eyes."

An animal groan started building in Lewis' throat, the sound of incomprehensible grief, and terror, and regret, and every one of the darkest emotions of human existence, of any existence, all combined into a single horrible wail.

The beeping from Lewis' heart monitor grew faster. His breath came in short, choppy gasps. He couldn't breathe. He was suffocating. The sounds of the room grew elastic, elongating and contracting, the volume rising and falling.

The doctor's voice broke through the swells of static pulsing in Lewis' ears. "I understand how difficult ... *sssssssshhhhhhh ...*

if there's someone we can call ... *sssssssshhhhhhhh* ... a spouse, or significant other ... *sssssssshhhhhhhh* ..."

The sounds of the room receded into silence, the way a passing police siren trails off into the distance. All that was left was the sound of Lewis' own heartbeat. His own breathing.

And then, a voice. His own.

"Give me that kind of luck for once, you know? Let me get two. One for him, two for me. Is that too much to ask?"

"Not at all," the disembodied voice of the bartender said.

Lewis heard the gurgling sound of whiskey pouring into a glass.

A double.

"To Michaelson," the bartender proclaimed. "May whatever luck comes to him, come to you, times two."

"Amen," Lewis said. The clink of their glasses resonated like a chime in a cathedral. "From your mouth to God's ears."

As Lewis drifted away into unconsciousness, one last thought slipped through the darkness.

Fucking Michaelson.

THE UNSCARED CROW

Cody Nowack

I lined my wings with the nightmare, its heavy, thick scent tickling my feathers. I could almost pump it into my hollow bones.

Almost.

As a crow, an unscared one, I had to chase the darkest of aromas and ride the filthiest of stinks. More often than not, they led me to who I needed to see--to scarecrows. Say what you will about those tattered bastards, but if anyone had the means to straighten an unscared crow, if anyone could spoon-feed us a healthy dose of fear--the main ingredient needed for a bird's longevity--it'd be those cornfield dwellers.

Don't believe me?

Try and keep up.

Wings outstretched, the sun cooking my feathers, I slowed as a field of green flecked with gold came into view. The stalks wavered in the wind, swishing, swaying, tumbling like the ocean.

The smell.

The nightmare.

They were here, right off the highway. At the Radley's farm of all places. Thankfully, so was a scarecrow. I could see him clear as day with my oil-drop eyes. He was standing in the middle of the cornfield, rearing tall as a crucified giant. His stick arms, pocked hat, and scrunched, burlap face all glinted in the sun.

Have it ready for me, I thought.

As I neared the Radley's farmhouse—a roof many of my brethren perched on from time to time--I started to descend. Without another flap, I sailed over the yellow taped area, the policemen, the medical techs, and the flashing red and blue lights, all the while taking in a lungful of the smell I traveled so far to reach.

Something had happened here.

Something terrible.

Something, I'm hoping, that will scare the feathers off my back.

Before flying to the cornfield, to the scarecrow, I lowered myself even further to drink as much of that dark, delicious scent as possible. It intoxicated me. So much that I had to land.

Settling on top of a rusted tractor, my talons *clacking* against the metal, I spread my beak and wiggled my tongue, inhaling. As I exhaled, my neck feathers ruffling with delight, I noticed two policemen below me. They leaned against the rear tractor tire.

"I've never seen anything like it," said one officer. He wore a cap. The other was bald. "Fifteen years on the force and I about puked my brains out when I walked in on that mess."

The hairless officer shook his head. His scalp glowed red, sunburned, most likely, and his pale skin had a papery texture. "Don't worry. I think I puked enough for the both of us. Just don't tell Kizler that. He's always on my case about that kind of--"

I cawed, then I took a shit on the bald officer's head.

"What the--" As his hand slid across his sunburned dome, as his eyes found me and connected the dots, he punched the air. "Get out of here, fucking bird! *Get!*"

I got. Not because I *was* afraid, but rather because I wanted to be, was ready to be. And for us unscared crows, that meant it was scarecrow time.

I landed on what would be considered the cornfield watcher's shoulder. He'd been around a while, haunted the fields for a few seasons. I could tell by the way he remained motionless as I gripped his straw and gouged his wooden arm.

"Well. Here I am," I said, though to those without feathers and beaks, it probably sounded more like, "*Caw! Caw-caw-caw!*"

As the scarecrow remained still, either out of shyness or needing a moment to collect what I had come for, I studied him. He wasn't anything special. He was rather standard, what with his button eyes, twig fingers, and tattered, decades-old coat that hung from his straw body. The only detail truly unique was his smile. It stretched wide, carving the burlap from ear to ear.

Almost like he was laughing.

"Go ahead." I hopped along his rail-thin arm. "Give it to me. You're the scarecrow and I'm the crow. Scare me. Tell me what happened at the Radley's last night."

The scarecrow didn't answer. They never do. Because they don't talk. They tell stories, passing along real-life horrors about the farms they oversee, but they don't do so verbally.

"Come on, spit it out. You know what happened here, don't you?"

To the untrained eye, the scarecrow wobbled in the breeze. But to an unscared crow, the scarecrow's number one audience, he nodded. Then, like they all do once they're ready to give the details, he vomited.

Chunks of stringy pulp and what looked like spoiled cream corn spewed from his mouth. I had to wait for the spillage to stop before I could check the discharge, but once it ceased spattering in the dirt, I immediately spotted what I was after: the seeds. There were three of them in all. Three black pumpkin seeds the size of thumbnails that sparkled like wet, rotted teeth.

Those were my story.

"Better be good," I said.

Gliding to the ground, I touched down beside the mess. I'd been given stories before. Not that any of them had worked and terrified me, but if nothing else, I at least knew what I was looking at. The amount, three, told me the story took place over three days--three nights, actually, seeing as the seeds were black. And their size, not big, not small, spoke of the tale's length.

Cocking my head, standing in the scarecrow's shadow, I snatched one of the seeds out of the mushy pile, choking it down along with a bit of pulp. It tasted moldy, damp, and unpleasant. But as soon as I felt the bits of seed and slime reach my belly, the story took shape, pulling me in.

Frank Radley pinched his wife, Mary, on her behind as she set two plates on the dinner table.

"Hands off, Mister. You had your fun earlier. Now make yourself useful and give me a hand."

"You're the boss," said Frank, though he gave his wife another squeeze as he passed her on his way to the kitchen.

Once the table was set, Frank and Mary sat across from each other. Lines furrowed their faces, gray specks peppered their hair, proof the last two decades of their marriage were spent working long days in the sun, on the farm.

After saying grace, and after piling his plate with pot roast, the potatoes, carrots, and meat chunks swimming in sauce, Frank said, "Can I have some of our crop?"

Mary plunged the tongs into the pot on her left, fishing out an ear of corn. As she reached to place it on her husband's plate, her silver, heart-shaped locket dangling from her neck, steam sifted off the yellow-white kernels.

"This year's producing some honkers," said Frank.

Mary dimpled her cheeks, then served herself an ear. "Might be some of our biggest yet."

For the next minute or two, neither Frank nor Mary said anything. Then, while chewing a mouthful of potatoes, Frank said, "Oh, I almost forgot. My doctor left a message on our machine earlier, something about needing to move my appointment to next Friday. Any chance you know which appointment that kook's talking about?"

Mary chewed a carrot. "Your colonoscopy. The one you were supposed to get last year when you turned fifty but didn't."

"Ah." Frank chased his food with a swallow of beer. "That appointment. Any chance I can postpone it another year?"

Mary pointed her fork at Frank as though it were a knife. "You can. But If you do, you're going to force me to give you one. And as much as I'd be punishing myself, I'll try my darndest to ensure you're punished more."

She winked.

Frank chuckled.

"Understood," said Frank. He reached for the butter. "Though on the off chance I do cancel, I guess now's a good time to oil up the shoots for you. Wouldn't want your fingers to get stuck."

Mary rolled her eyes. "Just eat your food. God, sometimes I don't know how I let you out of the house."

Lathering his corn with a healthy smear of butter, Frank, still chuckling, pierced the ends of the ear with his skewers. He blew on it, then sank his teeth into the kernels. He chewed only once before dropping the cob.

"Frank? Something wrong?"

Coughing, his face purpling, Frank spat several times into his cloth napkin, gagging on and off. When the fit subsided, he rose from his chair, pounding a fist on the table, a hit that echoed loud as a gunshot.

"What did you do to the corn?"

"What do you mean?" Mary's expression teetered between shock and anger. "I boiled it. Like always."

Frank guzzled the rest of his beer, swished it, then spat it back into the can, wincing. As he grabbed the napkin, he all but flinched as he unfolded it.

"My ass you did nothing. You sure as hell did something."

"Frank Radley, what in God's name are you--"

Frank tossed the napkin to Mary's side of the table. There, clinging to the cloth, turning it from white to red, were the kernels he'd had in his mouth. Each one was popped, like a cluster of fresh blisters, and inside them, oozing from their yellow-white centers, were crimson droplets that looked exactly like--"

Blood sprouted from the field mouse's belly as I pecked it to death, the first part of the scarecrow's story slipping from my mind. Delightful as my kill was, fresh and rather easy, I nibbled bits of flesh and fur and intestine hoping to taste a variety of flavors.

But it was no use.

I only tasted corn.

Bloody corn.

"I don't suppose you know why Frank's corn had blood in it?" I asked, cocking my head, eyeing the scarecrow from the dirt.

Whether or not the scarecrow knew the answer was irrelevant. He wouldn't--*couldn't*--talk. If I wanted to know more, I had to play by his rules and eat another seed. And because I was intrigued, that's exactly what I did.

In one hop, one shake of my wings, I plucked another black pumpkin seed from the pile of pulp and decay. This time, though, to dilute the unpleasant, mildewy taste, I dipped it in the mouse's punctured stomach before swallowing.

Hmm.

Better.

"Frank, can we talk? You haven't spoken to me since last night."

Frank sat in his recliner, the TV on. After taking a long drink of his beer, he wiped his mouth with the back of his hand.

"What do you want to talk about?" he said, clicking the remote.

Mary folded her arms. "You know damn well what. The corn. I can't believe you thought I had something to do with that--whatever the hell that even was."

Frank exhaled through his nose, snorting. "It was blood, Mary. You know it was. You saw it. Maybe if you would've taken a bite of yours, you wouldn't be so skeptical."

"Fine, it was blood, okay? It looked like blood. Your breath sure as hell reeked of blood as you hollered at me all night long. So, it was blood. But that still doesn't mean I put it in there. How in the world would I even go about doing that?"

Frank clicked the remote once more, changing the channel.

"God, Frank. Do you honestly, in your heart and soul, believe I filled the corn with blood? Twenty-two years of marriage and you think I'd do that to you? To our crop?"

A moment of silence passed.

Then another.

Then, clicking off the TV, Frank flattened his lips. "No, Mary, I can't say I truly think you would do that." Frank's eyes darkened. "But someone put it there. As you saw, every fuckin' cob in that pot last night was bloody. I don't like thinking it was intentional, but what am I supposed to believe after spending my day out in that field checking our crop and finding not an ounce of blood in the others?"

"I'll admit, what happened last night was the darndest thing, Frank. The darndest thing. But we need to stand together on this. Pointing fingers ain't going to get us nowhere. Maybe tomorrow we can chat with the Johnsons down the road. We both know their boy ain't shy from trouble."

Frank nodded. After he finished the rest of his beer he opened his mouth, but before any words came out, something solid smacked the front door, twice, sounding like a heavy heartbeat.

Thump-thump.

Frank got out of his chair. "What the hell was that?"

The heartbeat thump-thumped again, three more times.

"Frank, get your gun."

"Way ahead of you." Frank was already reaching for the rifle mounted to the wall. As soon as he grasped it, he clicked off the safety, pointing the barrel. He only made it a step before the house erupted with shattering glass. The noise started in the kitchen, then it carried to the bedrooms, upstairs, and then the windows in the living room exploded right in front of Frank and Mary.

Mary screamed.

Frank fired.

And when the gun blast melted away, the sound that followed came from outside. It sounded like wings. Like a thousand birds were zipping past, flying not to something, but from something.

"God," said Mary. "Look at this."

Frank lowered the weapon. Disbelief painted his face. Broken glass covered the carpet, glittering in the light. Laying in the middle of the wreckage, their bellies plump as though they all had swallowed an apple whole, were pigeons.

Dozens of them.

Most appeared dead, their necks bent, but some were writhing, spreading glass about with unstable wings.

"How is this possible?" said Mary. She had a loose hand over her mouth. "I mean, look at their bellies. It's like they're all

pregnant." She shook her head. "I don't like this, Frank. Whatever this is, it ain't natural."

Frank placed his boot on one of the dead bird's swollen stomachs. As he added his weight, fragments of something yellow-white filled the bird's mouth, parting its beak as it spilled onto the carpet.

"It looks like bits of--"

Corn. The smell was getting heavier. Thicker.

Swiveling my head, I watched as the surrounding stalks leaned toward me. Strong winds swept through the field, the *swish* of air imitating a hundred whispers.

I shivered, ruffling my feathers. The thought of the birds in the story sent a tingle tiptoeing down my hollow-boned back. Frankly, windows were real bitches for us crows, too. Flying into one, especially during springtime when the world seemed to care about cleaning again, was quite common.

But to fly into one with enough force to shatter glass, well, that was a little less common. At least for crows. Same goes for gorging ourselves to the point our stomachs could tear. We don't do that. I didn't think pigeons did either, but I could be wrong.

Hopping, I stamped the soil as I skirted my earlier kill. The split-open mouse no longer appealed to me. But the worm wiggling next to it did.

As I shredded the rubbery invertebrate with the sharp edges of my beak, I took to the air.

Landing on the scarecrow's shoulder once more, swallowing, I squinted, straining my oil-drop eyes to see a few details I had missed.

Yep.

The windows *were* gone. All of them. The front ones, the side ones, the second story ones, too. All the panes were now replaced with plywood. And though I couldn't say for sure, the front door, where the *thump-thumps* originated, looked caked with blood spatter. I could even see a gray feather or two stuck to the wood.

"All right." I glided back to the dirt, landing beside the pile of vomit. With the rising heat, it had become a gnat-infested mess. "I'm starting to feel . . . *something.* Let's finish this."

As the black seed on top of the heap winked in the light, I blinked, cawed, then chomped down on the last bit of the scarecrow's story.

Frank sat on an empty bucket beside the burn pit, his rifle resting in his lap. The small fire splashed his face with reds and oranges as it gnawed at the pile of dead pigeons and chewed through their swollen bellies.

"Frank," said Mary from the front porch. She set the hammer she'd been using on one of the chairs. "I finished boarding up the windows. Why don't you come inside and I'll fix you something to eat."

"Something's out there." Frank stared at the cornfield. The night was windy. The stalks waved back and forth like a million hands, each one calling for Frank's attention. "Our crop. It's restless."

"It's the wind, Frank. I know we can't explain what's been going on, but I've been thinking. What if it's nothing? What if this has all been a case of bad luck?"

"It's something."

"But what if it's not? And if it is something, what do you think it is? Who could be responsible for the last two nights?"

Frank rubbed his face. Which sounded like him trying to smooth a surface with sandpaper. "I don't know. But I trust my gut. And it's telling me something's not right. Did you get ahold of the Johnsons?"

"I did. I called them while you were in the fields."

"And?"

"Turns out their son has been sitting in the juvenile center for the last three weeks. It's not him."

When Frank didn't respond, Mary lowered her voice, sweetening it. "Look, why don't we head inside for the night and worry about this tomorrow. If you ain't hungry, then we can go to our bedroom."

"I'm not tired."

"I didn't say anything about sleeping."

Frank looked away from the corn, turning to his wife. "You mean to tell me fixing windows, sweeping glass, and smelling burnt pigeons put you in the mood?"

"No, I can't say any of that did it for me. It's just that we both have been a little high-strung lately. So I figure the best way to get this mess off our minds is to occupy our time doing something we enjoy. Together. What do you say?"

Frank smiled. "I say I could go for some of that."

Mary held her silver locket in one hand, smiling back. "Good. I'm going to take a quick shower and clean myself up. I'll be ready in five minutes."

As Mary headed inside, Frank remained sitting on the bucket. He snorted as the fire crackled, shaking his head as though a ghost had whispered something half-funny, half-crazy into his ear. Then, after checking his watch a dozen times, he made his way to the porch where he leaned his rifle against the railing before walking inside.

"I thought you said you were going to be ready," said Frank, entering their bedroom. The room was dark, but the bathroom light was on. The glow seeped beneath the gap at the bottom of the door, as did the sound of running water.

Frank slipped off his shirt, shoes, and pants. "Is this your way of saying you want me to join you?" Kicking off his socks, he turned the bathroom door handle. Steam clung to his face as he pulled down his underwear with one hand and grabbed the flowery shower curtain with the other. "Here I--"

Frank staggered.

Mary lay on her back. Lifeless. The water pelting her body ran red as it disappeared down the drain. Her eyes open wide, she had an ear of corn rammed down her throat, the outline of *kernels wrinkling the flesh near her jugular, and another cob stuffed between her legs.*

"Mary? No. No!"

Frank gagged. Several times his mouth opened and closed, making sounds, noises that could be considered a combination of moans and groans and growls.

"I'm going to kill whoever did this." Bending, he grabbed one of Mary's limp hands. "I'm going to put a fucking whole in whoever--"

Frank gasped, once, twice, three times as the bathroom echoed with a wet, fleshly sound. His mouth immediately began filling with blood, which spilled down his chin.

Reaching for his back, Frank, slowly, stiffly, started to turn. The ears of corn sticking out of his backside, two of which pierced his flanks, no doubt deep enough to impale his kidneys, the other crammed up his ass, wiggled with each step he took. And as he spun a full one-hundred-and-eighty degrees, he found himself face to face with--

The scarecrow lunged at me. His twig fingers punctured my left wing, pinning me to the ground, smashing the back of my skull into his pulpy vomit. In his other hand was a knife-sharp ear of corn aimed at my chest. And as he brought it down, as I waited for the fatal strike to pierce my plumage, then my heart, I felt something coiling inside me, something with fangs that bit at my stomach, my throat, my lungs. What it was I couldn't say. I'd never felt it before. But it was slippery and electric and it made me want to caw, made me want to scream fire into the world.

"Caw-caw-caw-ca--"

STRONGMAN SAFARI

Mark Mellon

"Jesus, Ricky, how long does it take to cut a line?"

"*Tranquilo,* Paola, this blue flake's literally like rock."

Estevez chopped cocaine on a mirror with a long bladed hunting knife. Manchester United was locked in mortal combat with Madrid Real on a giant flat screen, the score tied, 2-2. Somoza puffed a cohiba. Cisco, his brother, dutifully topped off his glass with white rum and pineapple juice. Ruy Blas swiped his phone and showed Somoza another trophy, a fifty kilo jaguar with jade eyes and mottled yellow fur. Blas stood beside the dead animal in the jungle, a big smile on his thickly bearded face.

Somoza grunted. "And where did you bag this one?"

"In Nueva Arcadia with the others. That's where the big game is nowadays."

"Not far from our rebel headquarters, Comandante," Cisco said.

"If you don't count the mountain range in between," Somoza said to laughter from everyone, including Cisco, used to being the butt of his jokes.

Estevez set down a silver tray, long, white lines laid out on it. Everyone snorted except Blas. Paola cuddled with Somoza. They all cheered when Madrid scored another goal. A sour chemical taste permeated Somoza's sinuses.

"I'm not saying the hunting's bad here," Estevez said. "Caimans, jaguars, even spectacled bears. But it's nothing compared to Africa. There's real sport and danger, elephants, water buffalo, lions, hyenas. You take a chance there."

Blas scowled. "Does Africa have a beast with hands that rip you to pieces? Macondo does."

Cisco laughed. "You mean the mohan. Ruy, I'm surprised you believe such tales."

"What's a mohan?" Estevez said.

"A hairy beast who lives in the jungle and eats people, you dumb gringo," Paola said.

"You mean like a chupacabra?" Estevez laughed out loud. "Those are myths."

Blas swiped his phone and handed it to Estevez. "Does this look like a myth, *Señor* Great White Hunter?"

They stared at the picture, repulsed and yet fascinated like passersby at a car crash. Taken outside a shack in the jungle, severed remains lay strewn across the dirt, only recognizable as human by the heads, mouths open in distorted death grimaces.

"*Dios mio*, this happened in my country?" Somoza said.

Blas nodded. "I came upon their hut two weeks ago. Their people, the Atormentados, think the family somehow angered the mohan."

"I heard stories in my childhood, but I never thought there was anything to them. Yet you seem to have proof, Ruy."

"If you're such a good hunter, why haven't you bagged one?" Estevez said.

"The mohan lives in the highest, most inaccessible part of the Sierra Maldita in Nueva Arcadia. A team would have to work together to flush one out."

"Let's do it then," Somoza said.

Everyone stared. Somoza puffed his cohiba, an impish light in his eyes. Cisco understood Somoza well enough to adopt his decision immediately.

"An excellent idea, Comandante. It will be like the old days when we led the revolution."

"I'm game if you are, Aquiles," Blas said. "When do we go?"

"Now."

Somoza was notorious for snap decisions, but this took even Cisco's breath away. He tapped ash into a bowl, as always master of the situation.

"We've been in the capital too long, getting soft, indulging ourselves. Time in the jungle will do us good. And if some monster is eating my innocent citizens, it's my solemn duty as the nation's leader to personally exterminate it."

"*Si*, Comandante," Cisco said. "That's the simple truth."

Somoza regarded Estevez, sandy haired, bespectacled, coked up, too American for his taste, even though he was a useful source of foreign exchange with his drug deals and credit card scams. He pointed his cohiba at him.

"We'll need an experienced hunter. I'll expect you at the airfield at 0500 with the others."

"Five a.m.? That's only four hours from now!"

"Better start packing, Ricky."

The others laughed, happy to mock the pretentious Estevez.

"Ay, Ricky, what a shit eater you are," Paola said.

She fixed Somoza with her smoldering gaze. "You're not going to leave me behind? I want to see this monster too, Aquiles."

"*Por supuesto*, of course, Paola. Who do you expect me to talk to in the jungle, these cretins?"

After the obligatory uproarious laughter subsided, the party broke up. Estevez, Blas, and Cisco left to pack for the abrupt expedition into Macondo's hinterlands. Iron constitution unimpaired by rum, cohibas, and cocaine, Somoza forcefully made love to Paola before he lapsed into a brief, restful sleep, dreams of conquest delighting him.

Woken by his own internal alarm clock, Somoza arose at 0400 to shower, shave, and put on a clean, pressed set of fatigues. He ate breakfast, coffee and fried eggs and plantains with beans and rice. At the last moment, Paola dragged herself from bed, brushed her teeth, and put on her fatigues that she filled out to stunning effect. Paola yawned as she combed her hair in the jeep on the way to the airport.

"OK, Aquiles, you and Cisco want to relive rebel days. Boys will be boys, but at least tell me we're taking the Lear."

Somoza laughed. "Santa Perdida has a dirt airstrip. We'll use a bush plane."

Paola pouted.

"You asked to come, *chiquita.*"

The jeep passed through the airport gates. Guards in dress uniform snapped to attention and presented arms. They drove to the restricted, military area where a needle nosed PAC P-750 XSTOL stood ready. The others awaited by the plane. Cisco snapped to attention and saluted when Somoza got out from the jeep.

"All is in readiness, Comandante. We await your orders."

Estevez was miserably hungover, Cisco red eyed himself despite his affected zeal. Only Blas was rested and ready in worn, stained jungle gear.

"*Vamonos.* Let's go. Don't keep the monster waiting."

Everyone laughed as always. They got on the plane. Nueva Arcadia was over eight hundred kilometers from Ciudad Bolivar, Macondo's most remote and backward province. Buffeted by turbulent crosswinds, the trip took over three hours.

Paola and Estevez slept in the back. Cisco dutifully tried to stay awake, but his persistent yawning annoyed Somoza and he let him sleep also. He and Blas passed time playing backgammon on a miniature set the seasoned hunter brought along.

The pilot steeply banked the plane as they approached Santa Perdida at the Sierra Maldita's foot, the provincial capital, unchanged since colonial times. Heavily forested mountains towered around them, untamed, uninhabited by man. The airstrip was a red, vertical gash in the thick green jungle, outlined with orange traffic cones. The plane had a rough touchdown, but the pilot expertly corrected and they glided to a relatively smooth halt.

Sargento Rivas, the province's police commander, came to attention before Somoza along with thirty men, his entire command. He gave a smart salute.

"Comandante, we stand ready to obey you. On behalf of myself and the city council, welcome to Nueva Arcadia."

Bells pealed from the whitewashed cathedral. A crowd had gathered, dressed in their best, faces lit with bright smiles, ecstatic someone like the nation's leader might deign to visit their humble, remote town where no one important had ever come before. As usual Somoza played his part to perfection. He went among the crowd, embraced men and women as if they were his own family, kissed babies, and bent low to accept the priest's blessing. After lunch in the police barracks, Somoza turned down Rivas's offer of an escort.

"No disrespect, Comandante, but this is rugged country. Experienced men fall to their deaths all the time, not to mention animal attacks. Only a short time ago, a native family was torn to pieces."

"I know. Blas told me. That's why we're here. To kill the mohan."

"The flesh eating monster," Estevez said. "You live here, Rivas. You've heard of him, right?"

Rivas's mustachioed face stayed impassive. "The natives believe he exists. Comandante, let me send my ten best men with you. They're good trackers and know the trails. They can act as beaters, flush out all the game you want."

"Sargento, I want my men on patrol, keeping law and order. Just take us to Blas's base camp. Also, your platoon has a full table of ordnance and equipment?"

Rivas nodded. "*Sí*, Comandante. We're equipped just as regulations require."

"Then assign a FN Minimi and an RPG-7 from the armory. Have them loaded with the rest of our gear."

"Immediately, Comandante."

"Aquiles, what's up?" Paola said. "Are we going to kill an animal or invade another country?"

Somoza laughed. "You can never be too sure, *chiquita.*"

Three olive drab jeeps left Santa Perdida, up rough dirt roads with endless, winding switchbacks. They slowly ascended into the Sierra Maldita's rugged, unexplored heart. Occasionally they passed Atormentados on foot, dusky, long haired men clad in dirty t-shirts and shorts with staffs and machetes. They ignored Somoza even when he waved, brazen faces stony.

"Forgive them, Aquiles," Blas said. "The Atormentados think we were sent here to persecute them."

"Don't worry, Ruy. I plan to change that. Killing this beast will be a good start."

The base camp consisted of a few plywood shacks with corrugated tin roofs in a clearing at Monte Espanto's foot. The craggy, irregular mountain dynamically thrust skyward, three kilometers high. Gentle rain fell from patchy gray clouds that scudded past. Twilight came early and swift in the high country. Macaws squawked and howler monkeys screamed.

Blas snapped on a lamp. "We're tired and need to rest. I'll show you to your quarters. Serankwa will bring you food. After that, you better sleep. We'll hunt tomorrow."

Somoza and Paola were given Blas's hut, relatively luxurious with an air conditioner and DVD player powered by solar panels. Impassive like his fellows, a mahogany skinned

Atormentado served them canned chili with rice, smoky from being cooked over a wooden fire. Paola picked at her food.

"What if this is for nothing, Aquiles? Maybe Blas told us a story, like a fisherman about the big one that got away. It won't help your image wasting time in the boondocks hunting a will of the wisp."

"Blas doesn't tell stories. I think I'll go talk with him."

Paola frowned, aware Somoza had once more put her in her place. Somoza left without another word or embrace. He found Blas outside in a camp chair, huddled over a map, illuminated by an LED lamp clipped to his cap. Somoza pulled up another chair and sat beside him. Blas handed the map to him and angled his head so the light covered it.

"If we leave at daybreak, we should cover twenty-five hundred meters, even with Estevez holding us back. We'll reach the new camp, close to where the family was murdered. From there we'll start tracking."

"What about dogs? Won't we need them?"

Blas sipped brandy from a flask. "Dogs won't go anywhere near a mohan. We've got something better. Serankwa, my man."

"You mean the Atormentado who brought us dinner? He looked grim as death."

"He has good reason. His daughter wastes away from a rare blood disease, contracted by a spider's bite. Her only hope is treatment at Sacred Trinity in the capital."

"By Heaven, she'll have it, whether he guides us or not. No child suffers in my country if I have any say about it. Not while the one who gets things done is still around."

Blas handed his flask to Somoza. "Well said, Aquiles. I'll tell Serankwa. He needs encouragement since his tribesmen will ostracize him for helping us. Now I'll say good night."

Amid the nocturnal jungle noise, small animals' rustle on the ground and in the trees, giant batwings' flap, a jaguar's abrupt cough, a strange, loud piping arose nearby, a shrill squeak like a hawk's cry. Somoza clapped a hand to his sidearm.

"*Coño!* What in hell is that?"

"The mohan. I've heard him a few times before."

"Well, what are you so damned calm about, man? He must be close."

"It's a trick, Aquiles. The louder he pipes, the further away he is. It's only when his call grows faint you have to fear."

"Ruy, you describe this animal like he's supernatural. Surely you don't believe that?"

"*Quien sabe*, Aquiles? Who knows? We better sleep."

Paola and Somoza brushed their teeth with water from a canteen that they spat outside. They made love on a narrow cot. Somoza slept soundly with his usual, maddening self-assurance. Only Paola stayed awake, wondering about tomorrow.

Morning came with tropical abruptness, the sun's raw, red orb heralded by howler monkeys' shrieks and exotic bird cries. They ate powdered eggs, fruit, and coffee sweetened with condensed milk. The heat steadily rose. Serankwa led a mule loaded with supplies and the FN Minimi along with ammunition. Somoza had Estevez carry the RPG-7 along with his pack. Chest out, head high, Somoza hiked up the steep trail after Blas. Despite his resolute air, cohibas and champagne took their toll. He steadily puffed after a few minutes.

The forest canopy provided merciful shade from the equatorial sun. Blas took the point, rifle ready as his keen eyes scanned the trail. Despite her spoiled ways, Paola proved more than able to keep up, fit from endless Peloton sessions. Cisco had proven his hardiness in the mountains decades before. Only Estevez flagged, a gasping, sweating wreck whose plight Somoza greatly enjoyed.

The mountain teemed with animal life. Wildly colorful birds flew all around or perched on branches, macaws with multi-tinted beaks, aquamarine hummingbirds, and many hued parrots, long wings gracefully spread. Rainbow colored lizards clung to tree trunks. On a far crag, high up a tree, a spectacled bear swatted at a beehive, brown eye sockets starkly outlined by his white face markings.

Blas set a demanding pace. After a few hours sweating on the trail, Somoza gained his second wind and worked to keep up. Even with Estevez, they still made good time. At 1400 they reached a small clearing, near the mountain's peak with a commanding view of Nueva Arcadia. Wispy clouds scudded by, wrapping them in misty trails of vapor.

"This is our camp?" Somoza asked, only slightly out of breath.

Blas nodded. "I've never hunted this high up before. Serankwa cleared this space. The hut where the family was killed is just below "

A sharp breeze rustled the tall wax palms' fronds. Despite the sun's bright light, a persistent chill steeped the mountaintop, brought by the insistent wind that continually swept down from the Andean peaks. Somoza ignored the cold. He took his field glasses and surveyed the mountain.

Vales and crags were starkly outlined by the powerful Zeiss binoculars. A bare granite boulder thrust out near the mountain's summit like an impudent finger. A shaggy figure topped the boulder, two legged, broad shouldered, features indeterminate in the distance. A man? He turned and bent over to display engorged, purple ass cheeks.

"In the name of God, what's that?"

Blas used his own binoculars. The crag was bare. He looked at Somoza, his gaze troubled.

"You saw the mohan, Aquiles?"

"*Sí*, clear as day, tall as a wax palm, and hairy like a monkey. He even showed his ass to me, the impudent jackanapes!"

A half remembered childhood tale came to Somoza. In a rare moment of doubt, he clenched Blas by the elbow.

"This means I'll die, doesn't it?"

"Aquiles, that's a superstition. Remember, we came here to kill him, not the other way around."

"You're right, Ruy. I'm being silly. Let's pitch our tents and keep a watch. I suppose we keep a cold camp."

"Exactly, Aquiles. Don't worry, I've got good rations, power bars, dried fruit, and empanadas."

Somoza set up the FN Minimi on a tripod in the camp's center, locked and loaded. Everyone kept a two hour watch with an FN assault rifle, Paola like the rest. In the darkness, Somoza conferred with Blas and Serankwa. Previously silent as a graven image, Serankwa spoke in Spanish.

"A mohan is elusive like smoke from a fire. He cries loudly from afar and whispers when near. He's cunning and avoids men. Still he has a taste for our flesh, especially easy prey or someone who offends him."

Somoza laughed. "How can you offend a wild animal?"

Serankwa gave no answer.

"What he means, Aquiles, is that we need bait to lure the mohan into an ambush."

"My favorite tactic. What sort of bait? The mule?"

"A man," Serankwa said. "Staked out so he's easy prey, near the peak where the mohan can find him."

"*Dios mío!* I'm not a brute, you know."

Impassive as always, Serankwa's voice throbbed with emotion. "I'm making my own sacrifice. Everyone in my tribe will hate me. Do you hunt the mohan or not? Decide, Comandante."

Somoza was taken aback by Serankwa's stark proposition. Yet as the Atormentado had reminded Somoza, he was still the Comandante, hardened after decades of power, used to sending his closest comrades into battle in the certain knowledge they'd die. He'd never hesitated before and wouldn't now.

"All right, if that's what it takes. We'll use Estevez."

"I thought you'd pick him," Blas said. "I'll slip a sedative into his rum."

"Better than dragging him kicking and screaming, I suppose. You two are cold, even for hunters."

Blas shrugged. Somoza puffed his cigar. After their meeting, Blas poured white rum into plastic cups to warm everyone against the wind's chill. Already half-drunk from his own quart flask, Estevez didn't notice the powdered Rohypnol in his cup. He was drowsy after half an hour, out cold soon after that.

"Get the mule," Blas said to Serankwa.

Somoza stood over Estevez's prone body. Paola ran up, beautiful face distorted by concern. She pointed to Estevez.

"Jesus, Aquiles, you drugged him! And now you'll use him as bait for that monster."

Somoza shrugged. "It has to be done, *chiquita*."

"I know Estevez is a shit eater, but nobody deserves that. Ay, Holy Virgin, what sort of man did I choose?"

He took her gently by the shoulders and looked down into her luminous eyes from his great height. "Hunting's a hard business. You're upset and I understand why. You'd better stay behind here with Cisco while we set the ambush. I give you my solemn vow; absolutely no harm will come to Estevez."

Paola was about to argue further, but wilted under Somoza's penetrating gaze like everyone before. Estevez was tied to the mule, drool hanging from his mouth, along with the RPG-7. Somoza briefed Cisco.

"Hold the camp with Paola. Keep complete noise and light discipline. Man the Minimi and don't hesitate to fire if you think there's a threat. Orders understood?"

"Affirmative, Comandante."

Somoza embraced his brother, an *abrazo*, a rare display of affection that made Cisco blush. Serankwa led the mule up a trail, guided by his countryman's keen night vision. Blas and Somoza followed. Each carried a heavy Bushmaster BA50 rifle with a Zeiss scope. Serankwa had an AK-47.

They hiked up the sheer trail. The night was moonless, the stars obscured by clouds. Despite his best efforts to keep quiet, Somoza sometimes stumbled and had to fight not to loudly curse. The ambush site was by the granite boulder, a small, deep fold. Serankwa had already hammered a stake into the dirt with a chain attached, a leather collar at the other end. They unloaded Estevez.

"Good attention to detail, Serankwa," Somoza said.

The Atormentado flashed his first smile. "*Gracias, Comandante.*"

Blas put the collar around Estevez's neck and locked it. They left him to snore on the damp grass. Sarankwa led off the mule to graze. Each man took a previously designated position to lay down three interlocking fields of fire into the fold. They waited.

Hours passed. Somoza fancied himself still tough like his rebel days, but fatigue took a steady toll as he tried to stay awake. Phantoms seemed to emerge from the darkness, amorphous shadows that could easily hold a flesh eating monster. The sharp mountain wind blew continuously in his ears, drowning out other sounds, especially any faint piping. Somoza stifled his nerves and forced himself to stay conscious.

The false dawn's gray light vaguely illuminated the fold. Estevez still lay motionless. Somoza sipped water from his canteen. He needlessly checked his rifle yet again. And still time dragged by. At 0513, well after dawn, Somoza wondered whether to call the whole thing off.

Estevez came to. "*Mmmmmpppgghh.* What's this around my neck? Where the hell am I?"

He sat up and searched for his missing glasses. Estevez got to his feet and yanked at the chain.

"OK, Somoza. I know you like having a laugh at other people's expense, but this is going too far. I know people who can make trouble for you. If you ever want to make another *centavo* off me, you better let me loose."

Estevez threatened and pleaded, wept bitter tears, begged on his knees, made enough noise to drown out the mountain wind until he finally slumped into a self-pitying, whimpering heap on the ground. Somoza kept silent and vigilant, ears cocked, index finger on the trigger.

Amid the wind's roar and Estevez's cries, piping came, the merest, distant hint of what Somoza heard at the base camp. Alerted, Somoza shouldered the rifle and put his eye to the scope. Nothing happened but the wind's sigh.

BBBBBDDDDDAAAAMMMM.BBBBBDDDDDAAAMMM M. BBBDDDAAAMMM.

An AK-47's unmistakable guttural bursts were followed by a brief, high pitched scream, a mortal, animal shriek of outrage and pain. Somoza raised his scope and spotted a dark, hulking figure. He fired two shots at the center of mass. Blas opened fire as well. .50 caliber bullets streamed in from two directions, but they only further ravaged Serankwa's already mutilated corpse.

"Blas. Rally to me," Somoza cried. "We'll hold him off together."

"OK, Aquiles."

Blas sprinted toward Somoza, Bushmaster at port arms, but when he rounded a boulder fifty meters away, a long, hairy arm reached out and snatched him from sight. Somoza fired multiple shots. Bullets tore chunks off the boulder, but Blas still screamed and died like Serankwa before him.

Somoza was alone with the mohan loose and angry. He stood and looked around, sweat streaming despite the cold air, desperate, clueless what to do for the first time in his life. The piping started again, only this time loud and clear.

BBBBBRRRRAATTTTTBBRAAATTTTTBBRRRRAA AATTTT.

The Minimi chattered below. The mohan had stolen a march on Somoza and attacked the camp. He had to move fast. The Bushmaster only weighed him down. Somoza cast it aside.

Heedless of his own safety, he sprinted down the trail, huffing and puffing, the RPG-7 slung over his shoulder, desperate not to arrive too late. He came to a hill that looked upon the clearing. Cisco lay slumped over the FN Minimi, slashed to ribbons from the neck down.

Before Somoza could grieve over Cisco's death, he had to act. The mohan stood revealed in the clearing, a hairy, pig eyed giant with long clawed hands, at least 250 centimeters tall. Back to Somoza, he steadily advanced toward Paola. She bravely stood her ground, FN rifle to her shoulder as she pumped round after round into the monster. Bullets slammed into the beefy torso, but seemed to have no more effect than bee stings.

Out of ammo, Paola dropped the magazine and reached for another, only to find her pockets empty. The mohan howled with triumph and charged.

Somoza knelt and put the RPG-7 to his shoulder, the artillery already assembled, the propelling charge screwed onto the warhead. He lined the mohan up in the sights, giving him a good lead. Somoza pulled the trigger.

The grenade shot forth from the tube. A nitroglycerin squib ignited. An automated system armed the grenade. The activated rocket sped the grenade along at blistering speed. The PIBD grenade detonated upon impact.

The explosion blew the mohan to gory bits, body parts thrown in all directions, blood and pulverized innards everywhere. Paola was knocked flat by the blast. The noise momentarily deafened Somoza and caused a terrific echo that rang throughout the Sierra Maldita in steadily diminishing waves. He shook off the aftershock, dropped the launcher, and ran to the clearing. Somoza bent down, picked up Paola, and gently caressed her cheek.

"Are you all right, *chiquita?*"

She tossed her lank, black hair and stood up. "OK, I guess, although I better get checked for a concussion when we get back to Ciudad Bolivar. It's good you came when you did, Aquiles. You're a real *cojonudo,* a ballsy guy. Only look at poor Cisco, your brother. He died trying to fight him."

Somoza frowned. "I know. His firing alerted me. Cisco never once faltered. I'll give him that. He'll have a state funeral with all military honors in Ciudad Bolivar. We paid a heavy price to kill this monster. Serankwa and Blas died too."

"Ay, Aquiles. We should never have come. What about Ricky? Is he OK?"

"I suppose so. He's chained to a stake near the mountaintop so he's not going anywhere. There are other things to worry about. The grenade got the mohan, but didn't leave much of a trophy. The head's pulverized. All that's left are the claws."

He took a knife from a leather sheath, the same one Estevez used to chop cocaine. Somoza went to a severed forearm, bent low, grasped the stump with his left hand, and methodically cut off the long, curved, bone white claws.

Paola clapped her hands to her face, mouth wide in dismay. "Jesus help me, Aquiles. Is there no end to your macho bullshit? This is what you do while your brother's dead?"

"He's not going anywhere either, *chiquita*," Somoza responded.

He pried off another claw. "Each one is at least sixteen centimeters long and pure ivory. I'll have a necklace made for you. Use the app on your phone to text a message to Rivas to send a relief party with body bags. It's the best we can do for Cisco and the other poor devils."

Paola took her phone from a jacket pocket and thumbed in text. "I'm not sure about connectivity this high up."

"Don't worry, Paola, the app feeds to a North Korean satellite-"

"AAAAAOOOOOOOOOWWWWAAAAA!"

A primal scream of pain alerted Somoza too late. Another giant charged him, shaggy and massive, only female. Furry dugs swung to and fro as she ran, fangs bared, insane with rage and grief at her mate's death. Before Somoza could react, the mohan was upon him.

She snatched him up in a crushing embrace, dug her claws deep into his back. Somoza threw his head back and screamed. The mohan only squeezed harder. He writhed as the mohan clawed and crushed him.

Somoza still clutched the knife in his right hand. With a supreme effort of will, aware death was near, Somoza plunged the knife deep into the mohan's neck. The long, sharp blade severed a carotid artery.

Gore geysered from the mohan's torn throat. In her death agony, the mohan only clenched Somoza all the harder until his back snapped in two. Blood seeped from his mouth. He only dug the blade in harder, determined to fight to the bitter end.

They crashed to the ground and lay still, both dead. Paola stood over the bodies, locked in a tight embrace like lovers. She bitterly wept.

"Aquiles, my darling. Why did you ever have this insane idea?"

Galvanized by the explosion and screams below, Estevez yanked at his chain with adrenalized strength, heedless of his bloody hands, until the stake finally pulled free. He ran down the mountain, the chain looped around his neck, nursing his injured hands. When Estevez crested the hill, a grisly tableau lay before him.

Blood and guts were scattered everywhere. The Comandante lay in the clearing, his back at a ninety degree angle, arms wrapped around a big, hairy, female beast, both of them drenched in her blood. Somoza's handsome face was arched back, mouth open as if about to give orders once again.

Paola knelt beside them. She wept bitterly. Useless as always, Estevez was left to mutely witness the end of Aquiles Somoza, the Comandante, who despite his myriad flaws, corruption, and decadence, at the very end died a true hero of Macondo, his people's defender.

THE GECKO KING

Sam Fletcher

I wake before sunrise the morning after the crash.

My old t-shirt smells of sweat. It's damp, so the sand clings to it. I sit up, folding my goose-pimpled arms over my kneecaps, watching the dark ocean before me. Light crests in the distance. I wait until the sun has lifted beyond the horizon before I stand and stretch.

I'm groggy. And thirsty. But mostly groggy. My head pounds—from lack of water or caffeine? I'm hungry, too.

I wade out, struggling not to splash, eyes peeled for meat. Schools of miniature fish catch my eye, but I'll need something bigger. And slower, preferably.

My eyes sting from the salt. The wind chops at my concentration. Then, I see it. The flicker of a tail. The boy is big and blue and green and probably delicious.

But I take a step, and he is gone.

This repeats time after time all morning. Wait, target, miss. I kick the shallow waves and return to shore, where the white sand climbs my ankles.

I sit, not acknowledging the ample jungle behind me. It's probably full of fruits and berries for me to eat. But what if it isn't? I lie down. Then, back up. I rub my stinging eyes, then proceed into the brush.

My mouth is dry. My hunger, by this point of the day, is gone. But I don't feel right. My Vyvanse prescription washed with the plane. It's rare that I miss a day. At least I don't have any deadlines or intellectual work that depends on me to be able to function. But I don't feel right at all.

I pass palm trees, grass, moss, ferns—are they ferns? I'm not from here. I pass things plump and round, vibrant and thorny. Things I could probably eat. But can I? I'm not from here. What is poisonous? What is edible?

Dynamic layers entangle each other here. It's hard to walk. I trample over brambles until I startle out a beetle. He scuttles along. Should I eat him? I sit and watch him work. I decide not. He probably stinks.

There are coconuts above me. I can see them at the top of the trees. But the trees are tall. Fifty feet, maybe. Girthy, too. No way I can get the nuts down.

The sun is setting when I return from the thick. I lie in the sand, and my stomach rumbles. A few meters over a few lizards lie, too. They are brown and horned. I could eat them, I think, but I am tired. I am weak.

If someone came and tried to fight, I don't know if I could fight back. They'd probably beat me to the ground. Is that bad that's my thought when I'm weak? Is that crazy? I don't like feeling defenseless. I want my strength back.

I'll get a lizard in the morning, I decide. Maybe if my body doesn't feel better, my brain will.

I shut my eyes, but nothing happens. It's not as cold as last night, and the waves are calming. But I feel awful. I don't sleep without weed usually. Even just a few hits of my pen, and I'm out cold. Not tonight. Tonight I'm irritated. Tonight I'm sober. Tonight sucks.

In the morning I return to the water. The lizards are long gone now. Maybe they heard me thinking.

My back hurts. I don't feel hungry anymore, but I don't feel right. My weak arms bother me. I wouldn't be able to throw a punch, would I? Ah, well.

I dive in, and my eyes sting when I open them. The water is clear, but my vision is blurry. Below me is all kinds of stuff—broken shells, kelp, coral. But no fish. None big enough to eat, at least. None slow enough to catch.

I break for air, then return. I break for air, then return. I break for air, then return.

A crab scuttles along. He's thick, and dark brown. Maybe he's a girl? Why is everything on this island male? Maybe it's easier for me to swallow somehow, literally. Boys seem easier to kill, morally.

I gasp, then plunge. When I get near, he lifts his claws at me. He's trying to seem threatening. It's cute, really. I'm probably fifty times his size. I pick him up from behind and lift him out of the water. I swim him to shore, in disbelief that he doesn't try harder to get away.

When I set him on the sand, he's full of energy. He darts back to the waves. I run after him, ripping two of his legs off when I make contact. Now, he limps.

I flip him over, revealing the wide crest of his underbelly. It's a trick I learned for an article I wrote back home. He *is* a girl. Whoops.

I slide my pocketknife into the crease of his shell and split it open. His meat slimes out of him. I look around at the trees, the driftwood. No way I am putting the energy into making a fire. I sit, taking my time cracking him open and slurping every inch of his innards. It's fun. No, it doesn't taste like a good cooked crab.

But it is still salty and flavorful. And I'm not bored, I'm not tired, I'm not hungry, I'm not miserable.

I feel amazing, actually. I smile. Amazing, what a little sustenance will do. When the crab is finished, I throw his shell back to the ocean. I stand and I dance. I was never much of a dancer, but no one is here. Fuck it. I yell the words to the ether. Fuck it!

When I lie back down, I see my lizard friends again. I guess that's what they are, friends. I'm not going to eat them, I decide. At least not now.

I look out. The water, blue. The sky, blue. I haven't seen a boat since I got here. I haven't heard a plane overhead. It's beautiful here, sort of. But no one ever talks of being stranded in paradise. Marooned in Zion. What happens then? My corpse in Shangri-La is a corpse in Xanadu is a corpse in back-alley Gotham. Rotting, for my lizard friends to consume. No one knows how to find me. No one is coming. No one will remember me. No one is coming. No one is coming. At all. Ever. It's over.

My chin quivers. My chest heaves. No one is coming. I stand, look out. I sit. What the fuck? No one is coming. What the fuck! I look at the lizards. They don't care. No one is coming.

When I finally catch a fish, my fade has grown so you can't really tell it was ever a fade. When I finally catch a fish, I've been off my acne medication for fourteen breakouts. I don't know how many days. But I have too many polka dots to count. When I finally catch a fish, my beard has grown too, but I don't mind that. I like to let it grow. It's my neck hair that bothers me. I'm so used to shaving that part. It itches. But that's honestly the least thing uncomfortable about my body right now. When I finally catch a fish, it is already half dead. I saw it fall from a heron's mouth as it took off.

I swim out and retrieve it. It's alive, but floating. Whatever. It still tastes the same.

I return to shore, taking bites out of rainbow scales. I don't care to cook it. I don't care to skin it, even. I collapse among the lizards. They are geckos, I've decided. Big ones, too.

They don't run from me, but they do notice me. I lie on my back, feeling nourished and happy. The geckos lounge with me, making an odd chirping sound. *Peep. Peep. Peep.* I peep with them.

My biceps still feel that way they've been feeling. It feels funny to lift my arms. They're weak. I wouldn't be able to win in a fight. But I feel good. I feel lean. I still feel weak, but a peaceful weak. A relaxed weak. Relaxed in a way that I wouldn't be able to feel if I were strong. It feels good. It feels strong, actually. There is some strength in weakness, I don't know.

But I lie here, and the geckos do too. This is how they feel, probably.

It's funny, when I imagined surviving on a desert island— everyone does, right?—I thought it would be constant discomfort. I thought it would be constant hunger, constant thirst. Constant exhaustion. Now that I am here, I realize it is all of these things, but also none of them. You get used to it. Your hunger swells and dies. Your weakness turns to strength. You feel good, powerful.

This is how the geckos feel, probably. *Peep, peep.*

This is why they lounge. You don't actually need to hunt and gather all hours of the day. It's amazing how much excess I used to live in. I only eat one meal a day now, most days less. But any more than that would be too much. Any more than that I would feel sick.

Is this how they feel?

I never imagined survival as relaxing. I thought it would be constant work. But you can't work all day. You need hours to relax, no matter what. No matter where you are.

I'm relaxing. I'm feeling good.

The geckos are not afraid of me. I stay focused on one, not meaning to, but he's got a cataract on one of his eyes. Cataract. He's probably a he, at least. The geckos lie on this sand with me, peeping.

This is how they feel. Weak and strong, but relaxed and happy. This is how they feel. *Peep, peep.*

Surviving is boring, too. Now my body has adjusted to this lifestyle, and there's no one to talk to. Finding my daily fix, my daily freshwater, only takes so long. Then what? What do I do but watch the position of the sun. My geckos leave. Where do they go? Do they pay attention to me, too? Does the sun?

Goddammit, I'm bored. What do I do on this island? When will this end?

I have all of these thoughts here, and no one to share them with. I've trained myself to always be keen to small details for the pieces I wrote. But, like, now I'm not writing anything. But I can't turn it off—the small, complex, layered ideas I tailored to an audience. What do I do with them now? I will lose them in the void. I will lose myself there too.

I walk along the beach, around the bend to the feederliner. The rocks have torn at the plane's shell—it's debris scattered. After the crash I fled as far as I could from the site. This is the first time I've returned.

I start on a long sheet bent from the cockpit. I put my knife to it, and carve small words in metallic scratches. Just, stories. Of crashing. Of surviving. Of whatever I think about. Not unlike these words you are reading. Minutes in, and I decide this is silly. No one will ever read it. I probably won't even go back and read it. What is the point of this?

I turn and look around. I think about fishing, of hiking, of trying to find water. It all sounds so boring. I keep scratching the plane.

It occurs to me as I do this that I don't actually remember crashing. There's no one in the plane, but surely I wasn't piloting, right? There had to have been other passengers, too. It looks like it can hold plenty of people. I just remember is waking up here, in this. Doing this. Something terrible had to have happened for me to end up here, right? The pilot had to have messed up somehow. But where is the pilot? Was I the pilot? I don't remember learning to fly.

Where am I, even? I must be thousands of miles from home. Where was I headed? Why was I going there? I don't remember ever having a lot of money for a private trip like this. Last I remember, I was working for that stupid magazine.

I stop and think about this. It's so funny, what I used to concern myself with. Competing with the other writers, arguing with the editors. I wanted longevity, recognition. Now I'm carving meaningless words on a plane. What the fuck?

I don't stop carving until every inch of the plane is covered in these scratches. Long past nightfall, lit only by the moon. Perhaps it wasn't longevity. It's the first time my headache has given me a fucking break since I got here.

The geckos surround me when my stomach hits the sand. Cataract sticks his tongue out to document my scent. But they just chirp. They don't talk to me, and that's really what I want. I don't remember the last time I've had sex, either.

I've reached an understanding now. Coast Guard will never find this island, let alone a girl. Or even a dude. I just want someone to talk to, and I miss my mom!

I spit the sand off my lips. When my tears touch them, they taste like the ocean. Fuck the ocean.

In the morning I dip into the jungle and hug a palm tree. At the top are ripe coconuts, and I'll get them today. I press my feet on each side of the trunk and lift myself up. I inch up, bit by bit, and my arms become sore. I didn't think I was strong enough to do this when I got here. If anything, I'm weaker now. But it's going fine.

Halfway up, I lose my grip and slide down. The trunk's texture scrapes at my forearms. My palms tear like a rug burn. I scream and punch the trunk. That hurts just as bad.

So, I try again (I fall again, too).

When I get to the top, I sock the coconuts off like they are those punching bags that look like uvulas. Shit, mixed metaphor. Ah well—no Google out here. I watch them plummet, ruffle the ferns. But I stay.

There is a little divot here at the top of the trunk, and I dig my foot in and sit. The lookout is amazing. Treetops stretch for miles. The island is much bigger than I thought it was. I cut off a few of the big leaves to give myself some space. They waft too to the jungle floor.

I take my knife and carve my new thoughts, scooting around and down the tree as I do it. I'm not confident in every word I spell, and I cringe at this. A few commas are misplaced. I cringe at this, too. But then I realize that I'm the only one who will ever read this, so who cares?

I write the word 'encyclopedia' a lot. It's got a nice sound to it, with many diverse syllables. Six of them. Then I write 'fuck.' Why not? Then, I just write sounds I like. I scribe Cataract's chirp over and over and over again. Peep peep peep peepeepepepeeeepeeepepeep. Peep. Why not?

My letters stretch and make shapes. My shapes stretch and make pictures. My pictures stretch back into stories.

When I touch ground again, my knife is too dull to hunt with anymore. But my tree is beautiful, and if I could take it back I wouldn't.

By night I feast on my coconuts.

Day again, and I see a heron—or maybe an egret or something—in the shallows looking for fish. I scavenge about for a rock big enough to do some damage, then creep up and watch. The birds are better at fishing than I am. But I am good at scaring them away and stealing their profit.

In just a few minutes she—probably a she—stabs her long neck into the splash and pulls up a mouthful. I don't hesitate, and lob my stone up and over.

It decks her square on the head. Her neck snaps, and she flops about.

I freeze, unable to calm my battering heart. I plunge toward her, not following any sort of protocol.

But a fighter, she is. Her flopping is quick and alludes me. She's slippery, and darts to shore. I chase after her.

She doesn't fly, but runs in short bursts then stops and flops about screaming. My heart aches when I hear this.

I keep at her, but she is still faster than me and disappears into the green. I hear her rustling the leaves as I take wide steps over them. I catch up to her flopping against the dirt, and I pick her up. She does her best to escape my grip, but she can't.

Amazing how resilient these animals are.

I look at her, blood trailing from her beak. I look at what I did. I hurt with her.

I take a deep breath, which leaves me in short bursts. I twist her neck until it snaps the rest of the way. Then I drop her cold and she hits the ground heavy like the rock I threw.

I start a fire that night. A long, frustrating process. But if I'm going to eat her, I'm going to eat her right.

She tastes unsurprisingly like fish.

I carve her story on the base of a palm trunk and work my way up. Her name was Eliza, I decide. Eliza had been on the island for seven months, arrived shortly after I did. She summered on a northern island called June, named after her grandmother. She wasn't feeding for herself, but for her three chicks—Ensley,

Eleanor, and Emilia. Her nest was but a half mile from where I killed her, made out of twigs and seaweed. She had a partner, Rome, who helped incubate her eggs before they hatched. They took turns guarding the triplets while the other hunted. I draw her, and her family, and her ancestry, and her home, and her other home. I draw me, and her tragic end. When I reach the top of the trunk, I remove the leaves that block my view and look out.

By this point I have finished at least fifty of these hieroglyphic structures. I have personally styled a whole subsection of the jungle. I peer out at the trees I haven't yet touched. In time they will all look like these. Purposeless but beautiful. Meaningless but not to me. In time, the whole island will be touched by my work. In time it will be mine. I am the king of this place, this other dimension, this lost chunk of existence. A small piece of permanence.

Someone will come to this island one day, I decide. Not to rescue me. I will be long gone by then. But someone will come. Perhaps they will come the way I did. And they will know I was here. They will know. In ways they never would from some magazine. A little bit of forever.

At night I return to my bed. My geckos surround me, and it feels familiar. It feels ok. The night is calm, the sky is clear. The waves crash at the shoreline. No one is coming. I will wake up tomorrow and do this again. You would think that there would be some sort of resolve to this story. I would come close to death but learn something valuable, or I would be saved and be nourished and full. I'm not sure any of that will ever come.

I look out at the stars, the moon, the horizon, and I'm not sure if I want it to.

Cataract crawls up my leg and onto my bare stomach. His tiny nails scrape at my skin, and I wince slightly but otherwise ignore it. It's the first time he's done this. He lay his belly on my chest and falls asleep. And I do too.

BIRTH STORY

Taryn Martinez

The invitation laid accusingly on the floor of our burrow.

"I've been invited to Bethalzgruub's babies shower," I said, examining it. It was silk embroidered on a blue heron skin that had been stretched and treated to paper thinness. Delicate, impractical, and probably cost more than what I made in a month.

"Who?" said Vezuubit, from the other room.

"Bethalzgruub," I said. "You know, the one from work? The one who lived abroad for a while and always finds a way to bring it up in conversation?"

"Hmm," said Vezuubit.

With the claw of my rightmost forelimb, I placed the invitation onto the table. "We've gone out to dinner with her and her broodpartner before, remember? He works under Wall Street. They're both insufferable."

"Oh, right... Didn't she just have a brood last breeding cycle?"

"Yeah. She said that one was going to be her last, but they were so easy she figured she'd have more," I said, very, very nonchalantly. My claw was caught on some of the silk of the invitation.

Vezuubit crept over and looked carefully into two of my eyes.

"Maybe you shouldn't go."

"No, no, it's fine. I'm fine," I said. "Besides, she's been bragging about the new addition they added to their burrow for weeks, and I'm dying to see it. Uhuisatugmi said it's beyond tacky."

I crept over to the babies shower with Yintalzeet, from work. Yintalzeet told me it was her first babies shower, and she'd had her cephalothorax freshly crimped for the occasion; she looked really good, but I could barely see her underneath the gift she'd ordered the babies off the web: a gigantic stuffed bird still wrapped in the expensive golden silk it arrived in. My gift, a Grubshub gift card, seemed aggressively practical in comparison.

"I can't wait until I can finally use one of the sperm packets I've been saving," said Yintalzeet. "I've got the perfect one picked out, but my career just isn't where I want it to be yet. I just know when I do it, though, it'll be magical. My broodmother said that for her, birthing felt like what her body'd always been meant to do...like the fulfillment of a promise."

"Yeah, I've heard that," I said. I started crawling faster.

"One of my broodsisters had a labor that was 48 hours long! She said that she was offered frog neurotoxin to dull the pain, but she read that it delays bonding and leads to negative outcomes in the babies' future, like lower income, so she birthed naturally," said Yintalzeet.

"Oh, wow," I said. I could see Bethalzgruub's burrow now, just past the new playground. The three MTA buses stacked on top of each other was a nice touch; I would have had a blast climbing that as a youngster.

"I'm not totally against frog neurotoxin, for broodmothers whose lives are in danger or something, but it just seems like if you're young and healthy, you shouldn't need it. You have to trust your body. Sometimes the doctors want to give you neurotoxin just to hurry you up! That's what my broodmother says, anyway. Did you use frog neurotoxin for yours?"

I could have predicted she would ask me about my birthing--they always did--but a cold shock, followed by a warm flush that reached to the tips of my scopulae, gripped me.

"Well--"

I was saved by the rolling away of the burrow's entrance rock.

"Oh, Bethalzgruub! You're absolutely glowing!" gushed Yintalzeet, attention diverted.

The orange, pulsating glow from Bethalzgruub's abdomen was indeed blinding. She fluttered her pedipalps and covered up with a crosshatch woven silk shawl, pleased.

"Welcome, girls! Please come in, we're just mingling before opening gifts," Bethalzgruub said. She took Yintalzeet's stuffed bird with a click and my gift card with a much softer click.

Inside the burrow was spacious, dark, and warm; clustered about were a dozen other giant spiders from work and the local broodmothers' group from Carapacebook, drinking from webbed bowls interwoven with live fireflies. Like Bethalzgruub's glowing pregnant belly, I found the effect beautiful in an annoying way.

Bethalzgruub took the place of honor in a silken nest, while her broodmother and two of her broodsisters hovered around her, proffering an unwrapped human thigh, a webbed drinking bowl, and a wooden serving tray of titan beetle canapes, all of which were rejected in turn. Yintalzeet left me standing in the entranceway and raced over to join the group of attendants.

I took a breath in, held it for a count of three, and released it. I told myself that I would stay until the gifts were opened. If I stayed until the gifts were opened, I showed that I was happy and normal. I crept over to join the group from work.

"Did you read that article in the Times about heavy metals in humans?" Zhuumyal was saying. Nods and *tsks* all around. "How awful. I hate thinking of what my babies are putting in their bodies when they eat. You have to be so vigilant."

"Oh, you simply *must* lay your brood in a vegan human," said Bethalzgruub. "Do you know the amount of toxic chemicals in a non-vegan, much less heavy metals? I mean, I know some broodmothers do that, but I just didn't feel right exposing my babies in ova to things like growth hormones. It's been linked to depression."

I tried, but I couldn't help rolling at least eight of my 12 eyes.

"We've had our vegan stewing for weeks," said Bethalzgruub, gesturing through the burrow to the nursery tunnel. The silk-covered vegan was currently cemented to its dripping wall which, I noted, was as impressively tacky as Uhuisatugmi had said: other food stuck easily to the ceiling and floor, along with the huge pillowy nest for the babies.

"Aren't vegans a little too lean for young babies?" asked Yintalzeet. "My broodmother says that babies who don't eat fat in the first 10 days won't grow up to have big broods themselves."

I winced. This was an old broodmother's tale that had recently been debunked. It had been all over Carapacebook. But Yintalzeet wasn't a broodmother yet.

"Oh, honeybee," said Bethalzgruub, joyously pitying. "It's actually all about the macronutrients. In the old days they'd pick any old human behind the grocery store, but I put in the extra hunting time to ensure the BMI of this vegan was a perfect 20, which provides an ideal balance of macros. You really can taste the difference--not that I would have any, it's all for the babies!"

The others clicked their chelicerae in agreement. With Yintalzeet properly chastised, Bethalzgruub settled deeper into her nest.

"Anyway, it's all part of my birth story for this brood," she continued. "I'm doing an oral history with the cicadas under the Y--they train them to sing in this really beautiful harmony that you can record and then play for your babies as they get older. I want them to know they entered this world surrounded by love, in a low-stress natural birthing in our own burrow, with just me and Thrarrgruuk, and were nourished with healthy foods from the beginning. That's important to me."

Everyone clicked in appreciation.

"I'm so jealous, Bethalzgruub. I had to go to the hospital for my last brood. At least they let me bring my doula," sighed Zhuumyal. "She coached me through the whole thing. I just wish we had been able to use the osprey nest we had rented specifically for the birth."

"You need to do more tantric web-spinning," said Bethalzgruub. "It keeps the ligaments nice and loose, and reduces the need for medical intervention by 14%."

"I read that it can even help increase the chances of a natural epigyne birth after an oviductomy," said Zhuumyal. "Of course, they say once you've had one oviductomy, your likelihood for another just shoots right up."

I tensed, as if for a slap.

"Do you think you'll try again, Mangarelzar? For a natural birthing, I mean?" said Bethalzgruub.

The lies were on the tip of my labium from long practice: the birthing was fine, the babies were fine, I was fine. We were always going to have a hospital birth because Vezuubit just felt more comfortable with it, and unfortunately I had some complications, but that didn't matter because the babies were born healthy and happy.

As I started to speak, I watched the many, many eyes around the room gleam eager, anticipatory; their owners vibrated with the desire to share their own perfect experiences.

All except one: little Yintalzeet, who looked at me with genuine shining excitable curiosity, Yintalzeet who only knew what others had told her and others never told you the raw screaming horror of it all, Yintalzeet who had never been reduced to an animal lump of reactions to stimuli, Yintalzeet who wasn't aware that the scrim between our lives and deaths wasn't just thin, it was transparent, and that even if everything *went* okay, that didn't *make* it okay.

Yintalzeet had no idea what birthing could be like because no one had told her. Just like no one had told me.

The pressure building inside my chest felt like stones crushing me, a burrow collapse. My fangs barely moved, but my voice flowed out strong from somewhere deep and dark and unstoppable.

I told Yintalzeet how I thought my birthing would be perfect, because I deserved it to be perfect, even though that sounds stupid now. I thought I could study for birthing like a web-spinning test. I read all the books, took the broodmothering class under the Y, even did a hypno-spinning class over the web. I was so prepared. And my pregnancy was so easy--no sore spinnerets, no nausea--I just assumed that birthing would be easy, too.

I told Yintalzeet that when I went into labor early, and had to go to the hospital, I was shaking the entire time. My plan for a burrow nursery birth was ruined, but I thought I could control what happened next. I tried all of the breathing tips, the stretching, the walking, that I'd studied, but the pain kept cresting over me, like it was something powerful and separate from me. I knew birthing would hurt, because I'd read that, but actually experiencing it made me realize how little pain I've faced in my life, for it to be this annihilating. I was still shaking.

I was hooked up to a few different tracking devices, which the doctors told me was standard. One of them kept beeping, beeping. The first few times, the doctor just turned it off. But after five, six, seven hours passed, and I hadn't released a single egg, the doctors realized my hemolymph pressure was high. So high that I was in danger, and so were the eggs. My body wasn't doing anything right, even as my brain struggled to stay in control, to think rationally; if you can't control your body, what can you control?

Eventually, I told Yintalzeet, it was clear I needed an oviductomy. A young, healthy spider, with no prior medical issues. A spider who did everything right. I never bothered to read about oviductomies during my preparation.

Instead I learned in real-time that when you have an oviductomy, they actually remove your silk gland and cut into your ovary to remove the eggs. Even numbed, I felt how empty I suddenly was-- just a body, and a body is a lump of muscle and hemolymph that my brain tricked itself into thinking it had power over.

My eggs were removed and implanted into a human in the hospital nursery, and they were healthy. All 200 of them hatched and ate and grew up to join the San Francisco colony. I was the one that wasn't healthy. I couldn't cope with the idea that it didn't matter that I'd done everything right during my pregnancy, because there's no one keeping score. Things just happen. All of the yoga and hypo-birthing videos and vegan diets can hide that, but only during the moments that don't really matter.

Guilt robbed me of any happiness over my babies those first few weeks. Because when it was all over and they were putting my insides back in, I knew I'd already failed as a broodmother. My body couldn't do this one thing that everyone else could do. What kind of mother was I, if I couldn't even give birth?

I finished speaking. The drip-drip-drip of fluid from the nursery ceiling echoed; the silence expanded to fill the burrow. The pressure on my chest had eased, but it was as though I'd just disgorged on Bethelzgruub's floor, or something equally embarrassing.

I had never said any of that aloud before, not even to my own broodmother. The pain was broken-fang-level tender, and I was reminded once again of how lonely it was to be unhappy. I figured that I probably didn't have to wait until the gifts had been opened to leave.

My escape stalled when a forelimb stroked my own, tentative as a wet-winged butterfly. Then another, and another, until every single gigantic spider-monster in the burrow was steadying me with a touch, all of us connected.

I could handle bragging, scorn, and judgment from these spiders, but I couldn't handle their kindness, and I felt tears building up in my eyes.

I couldn't see who said it, but a voice said, "I miscarried my first brood. No one in my line has ever miscarried. I felt so guilty, like it must have been something I did wrong. I still feel that way, sometimes. I try not to think about it."

Another said, "Half of the babies in my third brood ate the other half. They're only supposed to do that if they haven't gotten enough nutrients in ova...and I never wanted to speak about it, because it meant I must have failed. When I told my broodmother, she said I could just try again and it would go better the next time. I didn't want a next time. I wanted that time to be perfect."

Through a choked hiss, Bethelzgruub said, "This pregnancy has been so hard. I thought it was supposed to get easier. I can't sleep, I barely eat, and every time someone mentions how lucky I am, I scream in my head that this brood was unplanned, a mistake. But you're not supposed to think things like that, much less say them out loud. You have to be grateful, all the damn time."

Yintalzeet rested her massive, hairy cephalothorax on mine. I was scared she was going to say something about us all being strong warrior mamas, or making a web of something we were grateful for each day, or that next time would be better. But she didn't say anything. She just rested there with me, stroking my pedipalps. She was young and strong like I was, and her body would eat and sleep and birth, and we would all be there when her turn came.

"Let's break into the vegan now," Bethelzgruub said into the warm silence with a click. "I can always get another--they just opened up a Whole Foods a few blocks away. We deserve a little celebration, too. The babies will get theirs when they arrive."

The others busied themselves by pulling the vegan down from the wall and slicing through the silk to reveal its perfectly-marinated insides. There were more than a few wet eyes.

I sat by Bethelzgruub and Yintalzeet as the vegan was divided up. We were shy with one another until Zhuumyal started to tell a funny story about her brother-in-law who had been on a disastrous series of Webbr dates, including one where he matched with the same spider twice and didn't recognize her from one meeting to the next. Bethelzgruub laughed along with the rest, but Yintalzeet's eyes were still on me. I took a small sip from the proffered vegan as she watched.

I rested alone in my mind for one more moment, remembering. The pain of the incision. The disappointment in needing help. The failure. Those weighty things I had birthed along with my babies, and guarded in my shame, and allowed to grow fat 'til they threatened everything else.

I held them close, and then let them float away like spun silk on the wind, still tethered to me but a bit farther away now.

Then I took a deep breath in, one-two-three, and out, and turned back to Yintalzeet.

"Bethelzgruub was totally right about this vegan--I can taste the difference. It's delicious."

CONTRIBUTORS

Elizabeth Broadbent completed an MFA in fiction, during which her novel-in-progress was a top-ten finalist in the William Faulkner-William Wisdom Awards; her novella placed as a semifinalist the same year. With publishing credits in *The Washington Post, Insider,* and *Time,* she was a six-year staff writer for *Scary Mommy,* where she wrote about topics as diverse as breastfeeding and the Murdaugh murders (she liked the Murdaugh murder essays best of all). Her speculative prose poetry has appeared in *Bewildering Stories, Down in the Dirt* (forthcoming), and *AntipodeanSF* (forthcoming). Find her on the web at https://www.writerelizabethbroadbent.com, on Twitter @EABroadbent, and on Instagram @writerelizabethbroadbent.

Steve Carr, from Richmond, Virginia, has had over 600 short stories – new and reprints – published internationally in print and online magazines, literary journals, reviews and anthologies since June 2016. He has had seven collections of his short stories published. *A Map of Humanity,* his eighth collection, published by Hear Our Voice LLC Publishers came out in January 2022. He has been nominated for a Pushcart Prize twice.

CJ. Scuffins is a Communications Director from Dublin, Ireland. He has a background in journalism, theatre, film, and flash fiction. *Holy Mountain* is a new short story in his favourite genre of horror. https://cjscuffins.carbonmade.com/

Wayne Kyle Spitzer is an American writer, illustrator, and filmmaker. He is the author of countless books, stories and other works, including a film (*Shadows in the Garden*), a screenplay

(*Algernon Blackwood's The Willows*), and a memoir (*X-Ray Rider*). His work has appeared in *MetaStellar—Speculative fiction and beyond, subTerrain Magazine: Strong Words for a Polite Nation* and *Columbia: The Magazine of Northwest History*, among others. He holds a Master of Fine Arts degree from Eastern Washington University, a B.A. from Gonzaga University, and an A.A.S. from Spokane Falls Community College. His recent fiction includes *The Man/Woman War* cycle of stories as well as the *Dinosaur Apocalypse Saga*. He lives with his sweetheart Ngoc Trinh Ho in the Spokane Valley.

Warren Benedetto writes short fiction about horrible people doing horrible things. He is a full member of the SFWA and has published stories in publications such as *Dark Matter Magazine, The Dread Machine, MYTHIC,* and *MetaStellar;* on podcasts such as *The NoSleep Podcast, Tales to Terrify,* and *The Creepy Podcast;* and in anthologies from Scare Street, Ghost Orchid Press, Eerie River Publishing, Sinister Smile Press, and more. He is also the developer of StayFocusd, the world's most popular anti-procrastination app for writers. He built it while procrastinating. For more information, visit www.warrenbenedetto.com and follow @warrenbenedetto on Twitter.

Cody Nowack currently lives in southwest Montana where he and his wife own and operate *Bookies*--a franchise of bookmobiles and literary-themed bakeries. He has sold multiple short stories to a variety of markets, including *Every Day Fiction*, and has been represented by the *Cyle Young Agency.* When not barricaded in his office or running one of the book buses, he can be found hiking to the tops of mountains and, occasionally, on Twitter and @CodyNowack.

Mark Mellon is a novelist who supports his family by working as an attorney. He writes two-fisted, hardboiled, blood and guts pulp fiction and has four novels and over eighty short stories (many as reprints) published in the USA, UK, Ireland, Bulgaria, and Denmark. Short fiction by Mark has recently appeared in *Cirsova, Savage Realms, Swords And Sorcery* and *Weird Mask.* A novella, *Escape From Byzantium,* won the 2010 Independent Publisher Silver Prize for SF/Fantasy. He's a member of the HWA. More information about Mark's writing is available at: www.mellonwritesagain.com.

Sam Fletcher's work has appeared in Dark Horses, Eerie River, Simultaneous Times, the Los Angeles Review of Los Angeles, and elsewhere.

Taryn Martinez is a biology teacher and environmental educator of more than 10 years. She graduated from Brown University with bachelor's and master's degrees in environmental studies, with a focus on urban environmental justice. Her creative and educational work has been published in *Dark Fire* and *Competency Collaborative,* respectively. She lives in Queens with her husband Jimmy, son Conrad, and dog Abby.